THE COLD CASE

WATERFELL TWEED COZY MYSTERY SERIES: BOOK SEVEN

MONA MARPLE

Thank you as always to my amazing cover designer, Charlie, who fits me in her busy schedule at short notice and brings my vague ideas to life better than I could hope for.
I appreciate you, Charlie.
Thank you.

1

———

*S*andy let out an anonymous groan into the darkness.

Her whole body hurt. A pain started in her upper thigh and, every time she moved, raced all the way down her freshly shaved leg and up to the tip of her toes. Her toenails were painted coral, an ironic choice she hadn't been able to resist when she saw it in the shop. When she'd shown the colour to her sister, Coral, the reaction had been muted and disappointing. Some people had no sense of humour, Sandy had thought to herself.

She couldn't see their colour now, though. And she was grateful for that. If she couldn't see as far away as her own toes, clearly nobody would be able to see her.

"And relax." The instructor said, finally.

Sandy collapsed onto the mat, feeling the lycra shorts stick to her sweaty thighs and her sweaty thighs stick to each other.

"We'll take a moment for water and then we'll have a few minutes of relaxation to end. You've all done so well." The instructor's voice continued. *Her* breathing was under control. *Her* voice didn't sound at pain. Her name was Felicia Dove and if Sandy was ever going to have a girl crush, it would probably be on her. She demonstrated the most complex version of every yoga position, then showed how it could be adapted stage by stage, until finally she reached a variation that Sandy could manage. While not terribly unfit, Sandy had been mortified to realise how much flexibility she had lost over the years.

Felicia had a wonderful way of seeming pleased with every member of the class as she walked around the darkened inflatable bubble. No matter how easy the variation being practiced, Felicia would appear by Sandy's side and congratulate her, encourage her to stretch a little further, remind her to focus on her centre.

Sandy took a hungry glug of water, knowing not to drink as quick or as desperately as her body wanted to. She'd learnt that lesson in her first class. She swallowed, then took another swig. In the corner of the room, Felicia turned the lights on a dim setting and then stepped between the obstacle course of bodies to return to her own mat at the front of the pod.

Hot yoga, it was called on the flyers, and that was definitely an accurate description. Felicia set up a huge inflatable pod in the church recreation room, zipped everyone inside and blasted heaters into the already warm space. Sandy could feel the sweat pool underneath her chest, across her back, and those thighs were well and truly joined together in holy matrimony.

"And when you're ready, lie on your back and close your eyes. I'll play some relaxation music." Felicia said.

Sandy met her gaze and smiled at her between heavy breaths. Felicia was a fresh burst of energy in Waterfell Tweed, a woman deeply passionate about all manner of human rights who fit more into her days than Sandy could imagine. She was also a big fan of take-out coffee from Sandy's cafe, in her own reusable travel mug.

Sandy glanced across the room and found Cass, already flat out on her mat, her thick dark hair secured in a high ponytail with some kind of clip that made her look like an Arabian princess. Her skin glowed with the highlighter she regularly wore, not sweat. Cass didn't like to sweat. She'd give exercise a try but always seemed to exert herself up to the point of almost perspiring, and no more.

Once prone on the mat, Sandy closed her eyes and allowed the relaxing ocean sounds to wash over her. As each wave crashed against the shore, she let out a long breath. All too soon, the lights were turned up to full brightness and the music faded away. Felicia unzipped the inflatable pod and the women in the class stumbled weak-legged into the cooler temperatures of the church rec room with yoga mats and water bottles in their hands.

Sandy returned to a sitting position and let out a yawn.

"Did you fall asleep again?" Cass called across the room as she gathered her belongings.

There goes the peace, Sandy thought. "Ha ha, no I didn't."

Cass shrugged. "Just asking. I was ready to deny knowing you if you'd started snoring like last week again."

Sandy rolled her eyes. It hadn't been last week. And she hadn't snored. She hoped.

They walked out of the pod together, past a woman who must be twice their age and who put both of their bodies to shame with the sculpted six pack her cropped lycra top revealed. Another reason to be grateful for the darkness.

"Well done, ladies." Felicia sang out. She was all pixie-haircut, dark brown eyes, light brown skin, and a gaze so intense it felt like she looked through your skin right to your soul. "You're both doing really well."

"Thanks, I'm noticing a little more flexibility."

"I can see it." Felicia said with a grin. "And your posture is really improved."

A huge man appeared in the rec room doorway then, in a t-shirt that must have been sprayed onto him. His arms were the size of Sandy's thighs, bigger perhaps. He stood, leaned against the doorframe, and watched Felicia.

"Erm, you got company girl." Cass said.

Felicia spun on her heels and froze.

"Everything ok?" Sandy asked.

"Oh yeah." Felicia said, but she made no attempt to greet the man. "I'll see you ladies next week, I hope?"

"Absolutely." Sandy said, but she walked across to the side of the room instead of leaving, and pretended to fiddle with her trainers.

"They're just like buses." Cass said longingly.

"Huh?" Sandy asked. She kept a watchful eye on the man mountain.

"Fine men, they're just like buses. Along comes Bomber, and then along comes... *that*."

"She doesn't seem too pleased to see him." Sandy said. Felicia had walked across the room to him, but her arms were folded. There had been no warm welcome for him, no matter how impressive a specimen he might appear to be.

"Hmm." Cass said with a shrug. "Not our business, come on."

Sandy followed her friend out of the rec room after one last look back towards Felicia. The stern line of her mouth told Sandy everything she needed to know about how pleased Felicia was to see her gentleman caller, but as Cass said, it wasn't her business.

"So, fancy a quick drink?" Cass asked as they emerged into the fresh air. There was a slight chill to the air that was pleasant after the heat of the pod, and Sandy closed her eyes for a moment and enjoyed the feel of the breeze on her skin.

"I need to get a shower." Sandy said, then took a deep sniff. "And so do you."

Cass scoffed at her. "We all know I don't sweat. Come on, come to mine if you want? Shower there and then have a drink with me?"

"You can come to mine if you want?" Sandy offered.

"Okay." Cass said. "Olivia will be hogging the TV at mine anyway."

"I'm still so impressed that she came up with the idea to rent out the rec room." Sandy said. Olivia was Cass' younger sister. Her part-time job helping out at the village church was going incredibly well. In fact, the church had never been such a central part of village life before. Not for as long as Sandy could remember. Most weekends there was some event on, and every evening saw the rec room hired out for a different purpose. Waterfell Tweed had become a destination for people from other villages and towns nearby to visit. And that meant extra customers for all of the other shops, including Sandy's bookshop and cafe, and Cass' beauty salon.

"I need to change the shop name." Cass said as she glanced behind her to the shop front.

"Yeah, I've thought that before." Sandy admitted. *LA Nails* had been a perfect name when Cass opened and only did nails, but she had trained in all kinds of beauty treatments over the years. It was clear where Olivia had got her business brains from. "Have you got any ideas?"

"I'm thinking *LA Nails and Beauty*. I don't want people to think it's a new business."

Sandy stifled a yawn. The fresh air usually did a good job of waking her up after hot yoga, but she still felt like she could curl up and get straight into bed when she got home.

"Do you want to have that drink another time?" Cass asked. Sandy gazed at her. Her thick, spider-leg mascara was still perfectly in place. Sandy didn't know how she did it.

"No, no, come and keep me awake... I'm so tired."

"What's up? Aren't you sleeping?"

"I've been worried about Victor Dent." Sandy confided. Victor Dent was a farmer who lived on the edge of the village, alone, consumed with grief for the son who had died years before.

"Victor? Why?"

"I've been trying to get him involved more, you know, make him feel like part of the village again, but he's putting up a good fight."

"Maybe he just wants to be on his own." Cass thought out loud.

"That can't be good for him, surely."

Cass shrugged. "Your problem, Sandy, is you want to fix everyone. Maybe he's just happy being up there on his own."

"Maybe you're right." Sandy said.

"I'm serious." Cass said. "You've got every reason to be happy, Sand. You and Tom are happy, you've got amazing friends like me, business is going well, even your downward dog is getting better."

"You can't see my downward dog!" Sandy exclaimed. "Can you?"

"Heck no, I'm too busy worrying about the view I'm giving the poor woman behind me to try to look at anyone else." Cass said with a laugh. Her figure was trim and her behind was ridiculously pert, Sandy had noticed but not told her. She put it down to how much time Cass spent on her feet each day.

"I'm not unhappy." Sandy said.

"I know you're not. But you do have this need to find a problem, even if it's someone else's, and solve it."

Sandy shrugged. That might be true. But was community spirit a bad thing? Surely, it was good that she cared?

"He's out there all alone, Cass. I don't think it's okay. He's not getting any younger, or healthier." Sandy explained.

"I know that." Cass said. She let out a deep sigh. "And I don't disagree with you. But you've given him plenty of invitations, plenty of chances to come and get involved. At some point you have to step back and realise, he's made his choice."

Sandy shook her head. Her friend's words were true, she knew that. Victor Dent had been given the chance to integrate into village life. And the answer that his resounding silence gave was deafening. How had she failed to hear it?

"You're right." Sandy said. "I'm going to leave him alone."

Cass reached out and linked her arm through Sandy's as they approached her cottage. It was growing dark and the air was getting cooler.

"Hey, is there something in particular you want to talk about?" Sandy asked, only just realising how keen Cass had been to speak to her.

Cass tapped her lightly on the arm and laughed. "You just can't help yourself, can you! You've literally one second ago promised to stop worrying about Victor, and your mind's desperate to find something else now. Just be happy, Sandy. Everything's fine!"

"So there's no bad news?" Sandy asked, with a hint of a

smile as she searched in her handbag for her house key, found it, and unlocked the door.

The Cat sat on the bottom stair, glaring at the two of them as if they had stayed out all night without asking permission.

"Oh, I'm sorry baby!" Sandy cooed as she dropped her bag and scooped him up for a hug, which he tolerated. "Did mummy stay out after work? I'm sorry, I know you don't like it when I do that. Sorry, baby."

"Well." Cass said from behind. "I wouldn't say there's no bad news."

Sandy turned to her.

"You're apologising to a cat for breaking a curfew you don't have." Cass said with a shake of her head.

Sandy laughed. "Silly Cass, isn't she? I'm not apologising to a cat. I'm apologising to The Cat."

2

*S*andy awoke to twilight to find that she'd kicked all of her covers off the bed at some point during the night, which wasn't at all surprising considering the fact that she had slept in her flannel pyjamas and her fleecy dressing gown. She was toasty warm in her cocoon and for a moment played with the idea of sending a message to Bernice, her most senior member of staff, and telling her she wouldn't be at work.

What would she do with a day of freedom, she wondered. Her mind wandered. She'd start by closing her eyes and trying to return to the dream she'd just interrupted - a dream that she couldn't quite remember but, from the happy sensation in her chest, she felt sure had been enjoyable. When she'd slept some more, she'd fuss The Cat for a while and then pad downstairs and make a leisurely breakfast. Maybe porridge. She never felt like she had the time to really sit and enjoy a bowl of porridge. It felt like the kind of breakfast that deserved a person's full attention. After porridge, she might walk to the newsagent and fetch a newspaper and - imagine the luxury - actually read it. From cover to cover, every page. Although, she was in the middle of a mystery novel that she'd like to lose an afternoon in... so maybe the doom and gloom of the newspaper could wait.

Reading the newspaper was an activity that always seemed like a better idea than it was to Sandy. She felt the weight of responsibility on her shoulders to be socially active. To be aware of the bad things happening, even while she felt powerless to stop them.

No, given a rare day off, she'd ignore that nagging feeling that she should do something productive, and she'd finish her novel. She'd open all of the windows in her little cottage so fresh air would flow from room to room, and she'd wear a comfortable pair of trousers and the big hoodie of Tom's that he'd left one evening weeks ago. It still smelt of him a little and it made her feel safe and protected and loved, even if all of those feelings made her squirm a little. She was too used to being in control.

For lunch, she'd prepare herself something simple that reminded her of her childhood. A cheese sandwich, perhaps. A jam sandwich! Or maybe she could rifle through the freezer drawers and find fish fingers and potato waffles. Had there ever been a childhood problem that couldn't be solved with fish fingers for dinner?

After lunch, she might take a long bath. She had a lavender and honey bath bomb that had been in the bathroom cabinet for at least a month, which was unheard of. Had it really been so long since she had a leisurely bath instead of a quick, functional shower? The thought made her sad for a moment.

The daydreaming made Sandy smile. In reality, she couldn't remember the last time she'd taken a whole day to herself to relax. Her days off were usually full of the errands that didn't get done in the working week, especially since Books and Bakes opened seven days a week. She had no weekend, no set days off. She loved her little cafe and bookshop (especially the bookshop), but the daydreaming made her realise that she needed time to rest too. She'd have to book a day off to be alone and indulgently lazy.

"Didn't someone once say, *what is this life if blah blah blah, we have no time to use a bath bomb?*" Sandy whispered to herself. She couldn't see The Cat. He usually slept as close to her as he could, as if he thought he was stealing her body heat while actually he insulated her and made both of them warmer.

She let out a yawn. The sky wasn't even light yet and as much as she was enjoying picturing the lazy day she wished she could take, she wasn't tired. She picked up her phone from the bedside table - 5:20am, the illuminated screen informed her. She didn't have to open the shop today, it was Bernice's turn. Maybe she could enjoy some of her daydreaming plans after all.

Her mystery novel sat on the bedside table, a page corner folded to show her last reading point. She really had to buy some book marks instead of grabbing whatever receipt or piece of paper she could find nearby. Last night, when she had read three pages before drifting off to sleep, there hadn't been any scraps of paper. Whatever she'd used as the bookmark last, The Cat must have moved. It was incredible to her the things she could now blame on The Cat.

She had a theory about who the killer was. There seemed to be two suspects and one of them was just too obvious. Sandy was a true believer that life didn't follow the straight forward path. Always expect a few kinks in the road, a few unexpected twists and turns. Nope, it had to be the least obvious suspect. And in around 30 pages, she would get to see if she was right.

As she reached across for the book, she tried not to look at the towering pile that was her *to read* pile. There must be twenty books there, all mysteries that she had picked up in charity shops or ordered online. The local library had a pitiful selection of books and an even more pitiful selection of opening hours. The growing pile made her feel a mix of eager anticipation, and guilt that she wasn't reading fast enough.

Maybe Cass was right. Maybe she did always need to have something to worry about. Did other people feel guilty towards their books for not reading them quick enough?

The alarm sounded, it's shrill ring disturbing her thoughts of leisurely days relaxing and reminding her that she had a business to run. She yawned and climbed out of bed, spotted The Cat nestled in the blankets on the floor, still fast asleep. The Cat had a good life.

He opened an eye as she stepped around him, then returned to his slumber.

"Hold on." Sandy said aloud. She was talking out loud when alone with an increasing frequency but was amused by it more than troubled by it. She returned to the bedside and realised that the noise that had so cruelly interrupted her daydream wasn't an alarm, but the ringing of her phone. An unknown number. She'd let it go to voicemail. She didn't need any double glazing.

Although sales calls didn't usually start so early in the morning, did they?

She caught the call on what must have been the last ring, it had already been dialling for so long.

"Hello?" She said, breathless and ready to regret answering the call.

"Sandy? Eh, is that you lass?" A warbled voice came.

"Victor?"

"Is it you?"

"Yes, yes... it's me. Victor, what's wrong?" Sandy exclaimed. Victor Dent's aged, confused voice was unmistakable.

"Police are here."

Sandy's heart sank as she pictured the old man alone in his ramshackle house. "What do they want, Victor?"

"How do I bloomin' know?"

"Well, what have they said?"

"They're out there banging, I've not let them in."

"Oh Victor, you need to let them in. I'm on my way." Sandy said. She ended the call and tossed her dressing gown off her shoulders, then got herself ready as quick as she could, all thoughts of a relaxing day disappearing from her mind.

She sent a quick message to Bernice after all, advising that she would be late in or maybe not in at all. Bernice would manage. She was the kind of person who could lead a troop into battle, running the shop for a day wasn't going to alarm her.

The old car was cold, the cracked leather chilling her body even through the light denim of her jeans. She took a deep breath and drove through the village, past the occasional dog walker and a few cars. Her stomach churned as she drew closer to the outskirts. She could barely imagine what had brought police out so early in the day. Victor had nothing left to lose. His world had ended all those years ago when his son Travis had died.

She turned off the road and followed the track to Victor's farmhouse. A single unmarked police car idled off to the side.

"You're kidding." Sandy said as she drew closer. She recognised the face in the driver's seat of the car.

DC Sullivan stepped out of the car and looked her up and down, a grin on his face.

Sandy glanced down at her own outfit, to see that she had grabbed an odd pair of trainers in her hurry, and the big hoodie of Tom's that she had decided to grab, had a filthy coffee stain across the chest.

"Sandy Shaw, always a pleasure." The officer said as he approached her, attempting to maintain eye contact and not stare at her bizarre outfit.

Sandy crossed her arms to cover the coffee stain and stomped past the officer towards Victor's house, where she banged on the door. "Victor, it's Sandy. Let me in."

Victor must have been stood just behind the door because he opened it right away, grabbed her by the sleeve of the hoodie, and pulled her inside, before closing the door again.

"Victor, what are you doing? We need to let him in."

"I've done nothing wrong." Victor said, eyes nearly as wild as his hair. His jumper was as threadbare as it had been every time Sandy had seen him, and the quiet disarray of his life made her want to weep.

"Victor, the police aren't the enemy." Sandy said.

"Well they're not my friends. I know that much." Victor said, but he retreated down the hallway and off to the right into the living room. Sandy watched him, watched the sway of his arms by his sides, the protruding hunch at the top of his back, and took a deep breath.

She opened the door. DC Sullivan gave a terse smile that suggested he didn't want to be here any more than Victor wanted him here.

"Come in." She said. DC Sullivan almost managed to

hide his anguish at the state of the farmhouse. He was trained, a professional. He was used to seeing worse.

"Lives alone, does he?" DC Sullivan enquired, and Sandy's heart broke. There weren't many reasons a police officer would visit a person at home so early in the day, and even less reasons why they'd ask a question like that.

"He does." Sandy confirmed. The words *welfare check* darted across her mind, but that made no sense. If this was a welfare check, they were twenty years too late. The man, like the house, had spent the last two decades falling apart.

DC Sullivan took a slight cough as he followed Sandy into the living room. Victor sat in his high-backed chair and stared straight ahead, as if the officer would evaporate into thin air if he just ignored him for long enough.

"Mr Dent, I'm sorry to disturb you so early in the day."

Victor let out an amused grunt. "You're not a farmer, are you? This ain't early. I've already done the rounds and had two breakfasts."

DC Sullivan smiled for a moment but whatever darkness he was carrying flashed across his face again as he finally managed to make eye contact with the old man.

"I want you to know that this isn't my decision." DC Sullivan took a breath. His voice shook. "There's no easy way of saying this, I'm afraid, but we've had to close Travis' case."

Victor was alert, sitting ruler-straight right up to his hunch, eyes swimming.

"We won't be finding out what happened, Victor."

3

"*H*ey, wait." Sandy called, running out of the front door into the daylight. DC Sullivan had reached his car and turned to face her. His face was harried. What toll must it take a man to do his work, she wondered. He looked at her but said nothing. "What happens now?"

She saw him swallow. Saw his Adam's apple jut out as the bile passed it. "Nothing, Sandy. Nothing happens now."

Sandy clenched her fists. "How can you do this?"

"I know it's not fair." DC Sullivan said. "Trust me, nobody wants to make things harder for Victor."

"It seems like you know him?" Sandy asked, noting the use of the first name.

DC Sullivan grimaced. "I worked the case."

"Then how can you let this happen?"

"I don't have a choice. I take orders from those above me, and it's not fair him sitting out here waiting for an answer that isn't going to come."

Sandy's tone was ice. "It's not fair that he trusted you to do your job and try to catch his son's killer."

DC Sullivan shifted on his feet. "Sandy, the case is

twenty years old. There's no evidence that it's even a murder."

"You have Travis' body, can't you get evidence from him?"

"It's not that easy. He's been buried twenty years!" DC Sullivan said, his tone low. "I don't want to have this conversation with you. It's not pleasant. And I definitely don't want you putting these ideas in his head."

"How dare you?" Sandy asked, forgetting she was speaking to a police officer. "Sorry, that came out wrong. I'm out here trying to help this poor man, I wouldn't do anything that wasn't in his interests. How can you *not* investigate?"

DC Sullivan sighed. "The resources aren't there to keep up a twenty year old case. He's put his son to rest. That will be enough. I really think it will. As long as you don't start digging around."

Sandy shook her head in disbelief. "Resources. Unbelievable."

She stomped back away across the hardened ground, took a last withering look at DC Sullivan, and then slammed the farmhouse door to keep the world out.

Victor was stunned. He gazed off into the distance, seeing nothing, and Sandy stood by his side for a full five minutes without him making any suggestion that he knew she was there.

"I never thought this day'd come." He said, finally, his voice thick with emotion. "I thought the police were there to help. I never thought they'd give up."

"I know." Sandy soothed. She placed a hand on his shoulder. "Is there anyone you want me to call?"

"Nah." He said, and Sandy fought the urge to cry.

"Shall I get Dorie?" She suggested. Dorie Slaughter was

firmly in Victor's corner whenever his name was mentioned. Of course, she knew loss too, having been widowed decades earlier.

Victor shook his head.

"I'll make a drink, then." Sandy said. She rinsed a chipped mug until it was almost-clean and boiled the kettle with fresh water, and made Victor a strong tea with three sugars in because it seemed fitting for the moment not because it was necessarily what he would choose to drink. When she took the drink through to him in the living room, his gaze had shifted on to a large photograph of Travis that hung from the wall. The glass was thick with dust and the photo itself was dated, but the young man in the picture had a broad smile and his father's shoulders. It was impossible to believe the life was taken from him, that he'd nearly been dead as long as he'd been alive.

Sandy placed the drink on the stained coffee table and returned to the kitchen, busying herself with washing the dishes, then drying them, then cleaning the shelves of the cupboard before tidying them away. She checked on Victor throughout, poking her head around into the living room, where he continued to gaze at the son he had lost.

His tea sat untouched.

Suddenly, the front door burst open, and Sandy turned expecting to see DC Sullivan. Hoping he had had a change of mind and would be investigating, after all. Instead, an elderly woman with auburn hair piled high on her head, stood in the doorway looking at her.

"Who are you?" The woman asked. She wore a champagne coloured blouse with an enormous collar, and navy capri trousers.

"I could ask you the same." Sandy said. "I'm Sandy Shaw, I'm a friend of Victor's."

"Thought he'd taken up with a dolly bird for a minute." The woman said. "Well, where is he?"

Sandy gestured to the living room and the woman barged past. A strangled cry escaped her as she saw the photograph.

"Victor?" She said, and her voice cut through whatever fog he was engulfed in. She dropped to her feet and pulled him in to a hug, whispering desperately to him as Sandy stood in the doorway.

She turned on her heels and returned to the kitchen, where she boiled a fresh kettle of water and made more tea. When she carried the mugs through to the living room, the woman had moved away from Victor and was sitting in a chair across the room.

"I'm Valerie." The woman said, taking the mug from Sandy. "Victor's wife."

"Oh." Sandy exclaimed. The well-presented woman was a complete surprise, and she seemed unaware of the devastating news that DC Sullivan had just shared. "Pleased to meet you."

"And you, dear. Are you the cleaner?"

"No." Sandy said. It was fairly obvious, she thought, that there was no cleaner employed in this house. "I'm just a friend, like I said."

"Hmm." Valerie said. "Well, I'm here now, if you have other things to do."

Sandy looked from Valerie to Victor. "Victor, do you want me to go?"

"Stay." He barked, and Sandy hovered by the doorway feeling awkward.

"Victor, I -" Valerie began.

"Police have been out." Victor interrupted her. The words poured out of his mouth as if he needed to get them out without pause, without losing momentum. "They're closing Travis' case, Val. They're done."

"That's why I'm here." Valerie said. "I had the same visit yesterday."

"DC Sullivan told you first?"

Valerie shook her head. "There's a blast from the past. No, not him. He must have passed word to my local station, a wee grot of a boy came out and told me. I tried to call."

"Disconnected." Victor said with a shrug.

"I think it's for the best." Valerie said. "The case being closed, not the phone being disconnected. You really shouldn't be knocking around out here without a phone."

Sandy jumped at the woman's words. It's for the best?

"How is it for the best?" Sandy asked.

Valerie pursed her lips, not appreciating Sandy's input. "We've spent a long time wanting answers that realistically weren't ever going to come when it got past, what? The first month? Definitely the first year. At least we know now. This is as much as we'll know."

"They do solve old cases. It happens." Sandy said.

"Rarely. And the times it does just offer false hope to all those people like us, where it won't ever happen. They can't even say if it was natural causes, so how motivated could they ever have been to dedicate resources?"

"Resources? You sound just like them!" Victor said, his voice booming as he rose to his feet.

Valerie flinched then composed herself. "You can sit back down. You don't scare me any more."

"That's why she's staying." Victor said, pointing a shaky finger towards Sandy. "So you can't start saying I did summat I didn't."

Valerie let out a low laugh. "I never told people about

the things you did do, old man. I'm not going to start creating things."

"Look, I know that this is emo-"

"Sandy, it's not your business." Valerie said. She reached in her blouse and began to rub the thick gold cross that hung around her neck. "I had to come out Victor because he was our son. I thought we should at least sit together for a minute. And I don't want you fighting this decision, okay? Let him rest. Just let him rest now."

"I can't let him rest and I'll never understand how you can. You're meant to be a mother."

Valerie shook her head. "I am a mother. I'm a mother who knows when it's selfish to keep fighting. You're all about the fight, Victor. Is it even about Travis any more, or just you fighting and needing to win?"

"Get out." Victor said, his voice a low rumble.

"This is still my home." Valerie said. "I made it too easy for you, walking away and leaving you with everything. I wanted to have a fresh start, and I wanted you to be okay, but I'm still your wife and this is still all mine."

"You can have it!" He roared. "Is that why you're here? For a falling down house?! Take it!"

Valerie stood then and approached him, and Sandy saw the fire in her eyes. She could imagine the arguments they must have had, before losing Travis, when they were younger. Or maybe they were happier then, with nothing to fight about. Maybe it was grief that had tore them apart, splintering their connection like a bolt of lightning splitting a tree.

"This house is full of misery. Misery! I never want to step foot in here again." Valerie spat.

Her words were like a physical attack on Victor and he

collapsed backwards, down into his chair, where he held his head in his hands.

"I think you should go." Sandy said, preparing for an argument.

To her surprise, Valerie turned and left immediately, slamming the door on her way out. A few seconds later, Sandy heard a car engine roar into life.

She knelt down beside Victor, who was very still, his breath ragged.

"She's gone."

"She breaks my damn heart every time she leaves." Victor said, and he began to sob. "I thought, for a second, I thought, this is it, she's seen sense. She's come home. It's like I've lost them both all over again."

"I don't know how any couple would be strong enough to survive losing a child." Sandy said. "You'd look at each other every day and see what you'd lost."

"I can't lose them both and not even know why." Victor said. He raised his head and looked at her, blue eyes searching desperately for answers. "Why don't the police see that? Everything fell apart when Travis died. Can't I at least know how it happened? Why it happened? It's the questions that drive you mad."

"I can't even imagine."

"I know lass, but at least you try. That DC Sullivan, he won't let himself stop being police for a minute. He can't put himself in my shoes. And forget me. Travis. Travis deserves that, doesn't he? He deserves the truth."

"He does. You both do."

"Valerie, she found God and she thought that was the only answer she needed. I've never stopped asking the questions. And I never will. Even if it breaks me, I'll never stop. I owe that to my boy."

Sandy swallowed and remembered DC Sullivan's warning. But the funeral hadn't been enough. Victor Dent wanted answers. Victor Dent deserved answers. And Sandy would do all in her power to give them to him.

"Victor." She said. Her tone made a flash of hope pass across his face. "I think you should have those answers. I can't make you any promises, I mean, if the police couldn't sort it in twenty years... you know what I'm saying. But I think you should have those answers."

"What are you saying, Sandy?" He asked.

"I'm going to start investigating Travis' death, myself."

4

———

*T*hursdays had become pub night. It happened one week spontaneously, a text message from Cass suggesting they walk down to The Tweed to *keep the boys company*. Sandy hadn't been convinced that the *boys* wanted or needed their company while they worked, but she'd had no other plans. The following week, she'd found herself at a loose end on the Thursday night and so she'd messaged Cass to suggest they do the same again.

The Tweed was a typical English country pub, with older men propping up the bar as they supped a pint. The fire roared year-round apart from the rare days when even Waterfell Tweed enjoyed warm temperatures. It was a pub to visit in your chunkiest cardigan, not your finest dress, and that suited Sandy down to the ground.

She took a seat on the village green bench and waited for Cass who was, as normal, running late. She'd sent a harried text message full of misspelt words, asking Sandy to wait for her and hinting at the total 'mare of a day she had had. Sandy was fairly sure that her own day, starting with Victor's morning wake-up call, had been worse.

She appeared then, across the green, her luscious dark brown hair twisted into a plait as thick as a horse's tail, and hung over one shoulder. She wore her glasses; big, black-framed vanity glasses that she'd bought at a flea market. Sandy had laughed at the idea of vanity glasses but then had to admit how much they suited her friend.

She waved and Sandy held up her own hand and mimicked the gesture.

"Ugh, what a day." Cass said. She collapsed onto the bench next to Sandy. "I'm ready for a glass of white."

"What's happened?" Sandy asked.

Cass rolled her eyes. "I've had Olivia moping around all day convinced that Derrick's dumped her."

"Oh no, he wouldn't do that." Sandy said. She had a soft spot for Derrick, the pot washer at her cafe. "He hasn't, has he?"

"No. He'd left his phone at work yesterday, that's all. He did tell her that today when he picked it up, but she wouldn't believe him. She'd got herself too worked up by that point. She was devastated, Sand, it was awful."

"Young love, eh." Sandy said. "I've had a day and a half too, actually."

Cass eyed her through the glasses then got to her feet. "We need a drink. Come on, tell me all about it inside."

Sandy followed her friend across the road and into The Tweed, her eyes searching for Tom's handsome face without her even realising. He wasn't behind the bar. Bomber, the new assistant manager and Cass' boyfriend, stared up at the big screen. The pub was silent and tense, all eyes on the screen.

"Ugh, I forgot the game was on." Cass said. A man in a red football shirt eyed her.

"Shall we go somewhere else?" Sandy whispered.

Suddenly, the pub erupted into a wave of cheers and Sandy found herself grinning despite her heavy heart. The man in the football shirt turned back to Cass and lifted her from the ground, cheering drunkenly as he wobbled under her slight weight. He staggered back a few steps, losing his balance, until Bomber appeared and pulled Cass from him.

"You ok?" He asked her. She nodded, but the colour had drained from her face. Bomber turned his attention to the man. "What's your game, pal?"

"Hey Bomber, calm it man. Just celebrating!" The man said and Sandy recognised his voice.

"Gus?" She asked.

The butcher turned to her and grinned. His face was blotchy and red, eyes puffy.

"You look like crap." Sandy said. "Does Poppy know where you are?"

Gus shook his head. "Parents' evening. I only came in for a couple."

"Where's Tom?" Sandy demanded of Bomber.

"He went upstairs for a lie down, he's had a dicky stomach all day."

Sandy sighed. "So you've been serving Gus?"

"That's kinda my job. What's the problem?"

Sandy glared at Gus, but he remained quiet. It wasn't her place to advertise his drink problem. "He's had enough. Gus, get yourself home."

Gus looked from her to Cass, who remained behind Bomber, arms crossed, face set stern, then huffed and staggered towards the door. He barged through it and disappeared out into the evening air.

"What's the problem?" Bomber asked. "He's not on the barred list."

"No, he should be on the soft-drinks-only list." Sandy

murmured, eyes still on the door. She hoped he would get home safe.

"Oh, I'm with you. Got a problem, has he?"

"He did have." Sandy said. "He's been doing really well cutting down."

"Big game tonight, lots of people are letting their hair down. Might be a one off for him." Bomber pondered. He had scooped Cass into a hug and Sandy had to do a double take. It was strange seeing her best friend in an embrace after years of being single.

"I didn't realise you knew him."

"Me?" Bomber asked. "I don't."

"He knew your name."

Bomber laughed. "Perk of the job... or curse of the job sometimes."

Sandy nodded and followed Bomber and Cass back towards the bar, where a rowdy crowd had gathered, all wanting a celebratory pint after the goal scoring. The barmaid, Tanya, looked across at Bomber with urgency.

"Right, I'm still on duty. This'll all settle down when the game's finished. Stick around for a bit?"

"We will." Cass said as Bomber undid himself from her embrace.

"I'm going to just pop upstairs and see if -" Sandy began, but the door at the back of the bar opened and Tom appeared. His skin had a green tinge to it and he clung to the door frame as he entered. "Oh, man."

"And you said Gus looked like crap." Cass quipped.

Sandy went to him and placed a hand on the side of his face, then his forehead. He didn't have a temperature. She could hear his stomach gurgling as she stood by him.

"Wow, you're really under the weather." She said. "Come on, let's get you back to bed."

He shook his head a fraction of an inch then winced. "I've missed a goal, haven't I? I'll just watch the game a bit. What are you doing here? Are you okay? You look tired?"

Sandy smiled. Trust Tom, even in his own ill health, to notice the exhaustion etched across her own face. He truly was a keeper.

"I'm fine. Come on, let's get a table if you're going to stay down here." Sandy said. She took Tom's hand and led him like a child out from behind the bar and into a booth table. Cass followed, eyeing him warily. She had a love hate relationship with Tom and the two of them constantly bickered and teased each other.

"Don't get too close to me." She said as she sat opposite him. "You've not been eating at Books and Bakes again, have you?"

"Ha ha." Sandy said as she screwed up her nose.

"Sandy, are you sure you're okay?" Tom asked again.

"Oh yeah, you were saying how bad your day had been. What happened?" Cass asked.

Bomber appeared by their booth, loitering near Cass now the bar rush had died down.

Sandy took a deep breath. "I had a call from Victor Dent this morning."

"I thought he'd gone back into hiding?" Cass asked.

"Well, he had. He rang because the police were at his door. They've closed the case. They won't be trying to find out what happened to Travis."

"I didn't know the case was still open." Cass said. "It was years ago."

"Twenty years ago." Sandy said with a grimace.

"How did Victor take that news?"

"Well, how would you expect? He was devastated. All he wants is answers."

Tom reached along the table and took her hand in his. "It's good that he had you to call to help him."

"Well, not really. I couldn't get the police to change their decision." Sandy said.

"I don't know how they could possibly solve a case that old." Cass said.

Bomber shifted on his feet. "Anyone want a drink? Tanya'll have my head on a stick if I stand around 'ere without getting an order."

"Ugh, yes please. White wine. Same, Sandy?"

"No." She said, a little more brusque than intended. "No thanks, I'll get a mocha please."

"Anything for you, captain?" Bomber asked.

Tom shook his head quickly and Bomber walked away to the bar.

"You should drink water, stay hydrated if you're being sick." Sandy said to Tom. She rose to her feet. "I'll go and ask for one."

Tom protested but she walked across to the bar, where Bomber was measuring the glass of wine. "Changed your mind?"

"Can we get a water for Tom as well?"

"Sure." Bomber said.

"You grew up here, Bomber, do you remember much about what happened to Travis?"

"Me?" Bomber asked. The wine sloshed over the measuring cup onto the bar. He cursed under his breath. "I didn't know the fella, only heard what was in the newspaper."

Sandy nodded. "I know a lot of the lads hung out around Black Rock back in the day, thought you might have heard something."

"Nah. He was older then me, though." Bomber said as he

wiped the bar dry. "This is a never ending job, I tell ya, mopping up spilt drinks. Normally not spilt by me, though, if Tanya asks."

"Your secret's safe." Sandy said with a smile. Tanya was nowhere near as intimidating as Bomber liked to pretend.

"Go on back to the table, I'll bring them over." Bomber said.

Sandy smiled at him and returned to the booth table, where Tom's eyes were fixed on the big screen and Cass was furiously typing a message into her phone.

"Teenagers." She moaned when Sandy sat down. "Olivia wants Derrick to stay over now she's accepted his explanation. I've told her no way. Can you imagine our parents letting a boy stay over?"

"Well, no." Sandy said. "But I can imagine us... or one of us... pushing our luck and asking."

Cass' cheeks flushed and she instinctively turned to glance at Bomber, the childhood sweetheart she had just reunited with. "Fair point. I'm not changing my mind, though. Anyway, you were telling us about Victor?"

"I just feel so sorry for him." Sandy said. "Imagine not knowing what happened to your child?"

"Don't you think not knowing is better sometimes?" Tom asked, at least half his attention now on Sandy and not how ill he felt.

"Erm, no?"

"So what if something really awful happened to Travis. If Victor knew that, he'd never be able to stop picturing it."

"Some people die really nasty deaths, Sand." Cass said. Her eyes were full of concern under spider-leg lashes.

"I know that. But I still believe that Victor needs to know."

"And now he's not going to." Tom said with a sad smile.

"Well..." Sandy began. Bomber appeared at the booth holding a tray. He passed the water to Tom, the wine to Cass, and the big steaming mug of mocha to Sandy. "I told Victor I'm going to investigate."

"What?" Bomber asked.

"I'm going to investigate Travis' death. And, I need you guys to help. I honestly don't have a clue where to start."

"Ugh." Cass said. "You're allergic to a quiet life, Sandy, aren't you? I don't know what help I could offer."

"I'll do whatever you need." Tom said. His voice was quiet and unsteady and his stomach gave another, urgent gurgle. He sounded as if he needed to be closer to a toilet than he was. He gave her hand a supportive squeeze.

Bomber turned to walk away from the booth.

"Bomber?" Sandy called. He turned back to her, gave a smile.

"I just asked for your help?"

"Oh, sorry. I was miles away." He said, his gaze anywhere other than on her eyes. "Sure, Sandy. Sure. No problem."

And then he turned again and walked back to the bar.

5

The next morning, Sandy slept in. She'd drank no alcohol so it wasn't a hangover that made her so tired. It felt like an emotional tiredness, an exhaustion that started in her mind and carried across to her bones. She had no idea whether she'd forgot to set the alarm, or managed to turn it off without fully waking up.

Either way, when she looked at the time, she dived out of bed and got ready as quick as possible while The Cat watched with an amused smirk on his fluffy face.

"It's alright for you, Mr." She said as she almost tripped over him in the bathroom doorway. "Some of us have got jobs to go to so we can keep our animals in the lifestyle they're accustomed to."

She sprinted downstairs, taking the uneven steps two at a time in an unusual display of disregard for her own safety, and grabbed her yellow mac from the coat stand. As she bent down to pick up her handbag from the carpet, a sharp knock at the door made her jump.

Sure, it was late for her to open Books and Bakes, but it was early in the day for most people.

Definitely too early for social callers.

She opened the door and groaned at the sight of who stood on her doorstep.

"Can I come in?"

"I guess." Sandy agreed. She opened the door and allowed DC Sullivan to enter. He was dressed in casual clothes; a pair of black jeans, brown boots and a light rain jacket zipped right up to his neck. She showed him in to the living room, where he took a seat before being offered one. "Do you want a drink? I was just on my way to work..."

"Nah, I'm fine thanks. I won't take long." He said, then waited for her to take a seat.

"Are you back in town, then? For a while?" She asked as she took a seat across from him.

He shook his head. "I just wanted to see you. I did try last night."

"I was out."

"Investigating?" He asked.

"At the pub, actually." Sandy said. "I'm not a drinker, but the landlord's my boyfriend."

DC Sullivan nodded. Why had she told him that? She needed to learn to stop filling awkward silences with inane chatter.

"So?" She prompted.

"I just wanted to have a chat about Victor Dent. I do feel for his situation, I really do. But I honestly believe that the case being closed is in his best interests."

"It isn't." Sandy said. She crossed her arms over her chest. Her yellow mac sat draped over her lap.

"How can you be so sure?"

"Because he's told me. Everyone else seems to have their own ideas and agenda, but if you actually listen to Victor, he's speaking for himself loud and clear. And he wants answers."

DC Sullivan nodded. "I've seen a lot of people over the years who think they want answers."

"What does that mean?"

He sighed. "You're right that I have my own ideas, Sandy, and they're based on years of policing. Years of dealing with the worst kind of people out there. So I see things differently, I know that. And I know that the kind of answers I can give sometimes make things a hell of a lot worse, not better."

Sandy swallowed. "You have an idea what happened, don't you?"

"We never had any evidence or any leads."

Sandy sat in silence, waiting for him to go on.

"I remember another dad like Victor. Desperate for answers. And we got those answers for him. He didn't last a week after knowing."

"I don't -"

"Hanged himself." DC Sullivan said, eyes down on the carpet.

"That's awful."

"It was the nightmares that did it. He'd always had them, but they'd come from his imagination. As soon as we could tell him exactly what had happened, they weren't imagination anymore. He could fill in the blanks. He knew what his daughter had gone through. And that killed him."

Sandy gulped. She didn't want to put Victor through more pain. "That's so tragic, it obviously is. But Victor's a grown man, he should be able to choose how he wants to process his grief, surely?"

"Maybe." DC Sullivan said with a shrug. "I honestly don't know what the answer is. I just needed you to know that there's no happy ending for him."

"I know that."

"I always feel like you're trying to fight me, like I'm the bad guy, and that's really not the case. My whole life is about getting justice for people."

"I do know that." Sandy said. "I just don't think we see eye to eye on everything."

He nodded. "I'll agree with that. And that's to be expected."

"So, this is it? You came to chat with me?"

"Pretty much." DC Sullivan said. He gestured to his boots. "I'm not even here as an officer, really. Just a concerned citizen."

"I promised Victor that I'm going to look into it. I can't break that promise."

DC Sullivan took a long, slow breath and nodded. "I thought you'd say that."

Sandy smiled. The officer was learning not to underestimate her, it seemed. She may have first met him as a naive young woman, but she had blossomed into confidence.

"So, since you're here, can you tell me anything that might help me?"

DC Sullivan laughed and scratched his ear. "I don't know much, to be honest."

"You said you worked the case?"

"Yeah, twenty years ago, I was making coffees and shadowing the real cops. I didn't have any real involvement."

"Who did? Maybe I could speak to them?"

"I doubt it. The DCI's retired. May even be dead now. He moved areas, left under a cloud."

"What was his name?"

DC Sullivan sighed. "I'm only telling you what's public record, alright? You could get this stuff from the library archives. His name was Simmons. Archie Simmons. You won't find him, though. There's more than you looking for him."

"What did he do?"

"Nothing in this case." DC Sullivan said. "Listen, I've given you my warning about how this could end for Victor, I don't want to keep you. You said you're going to work?"

"That can wait." Sandy said. She picked her phone up from her handbag and punched in a message to Bernice. "This is important. If the DCI wasn't above board…"

"I never said that." DC Sullivan said. "There was an investigation. He left before it was finished. So, officially, nothing was proved."

"But there was an investigation." Sandy said. "What was it for? Was he bent?"

"You know I'm not going to answer that." DC Sullivan said. She'd expected that answer. "But go to the library archives if you're that interested. It was nothing to do with this case."

"I'll look into it." Sandy said. "You don't have any idea where I could find the guy to talk to? I'd rather do that than rely on what a journalist had to say."

DC Sullivan shook his head. "I honestly don't. I was hardly friends with the guy, he could have been my dad. He left and that was the end of him as far as I was concerned."

"Okay. Well, I guess tracking him down could be a first step. I mean, did the guy investigate the case much? He must know something, right?"

DC Sullivan groaned and stood up from the chair. He walked across to the window and gazed out. "Sandy, you're really going down a road you might not want to go down."

"You keep saying that but then tell me you don't know anything. Both of those things can't be true."

"They are." DC Sullivan said as he looked through the

small window. School children were starting to walk by with parents, harried mothers attempted to hold hands with primary aged children while pushing pushchairs and carrying lunchboxes and, in some cases, talking on mobile phones. "There was no evidence, but as an officer you start to get hunches. You can't charge a person based on a hunch, doesn't matter how experienced you are. There has to be evidence."

"So you had a hunch?"

"Not me. Like I say, I was too junior. I wouldn't have recognised a hunch if one had come and hit me in the face. Not then. But I heard talk. The others had a hunch."

"Okaaaaay." She said in a long, drawn-out breath.

DC Sullivan sighed. "Word on the beat was it was the mother."

"Valerie?" Sandy asked.

"I don't know her name." DC Sullivan said with a shrug and a shake of his head. He turned and faced her, his expression grim. The light poring in the window was brighter now, and the quiet road was relatively busy with slow-moving cars and fast-moving children. The morning rush. "Just be careful what you're poking around into, eh?"

"But why her? Was she interviewed?"

"Sandy, I can't tell you all this. I'm just saying, it might not be the answer that Victor wants."

Sandy bit her lip and looked across at the officer. They'd had their differences, in fact it seemed that they never saw eye to eye.

"Let me be really clear on something. The case has been closed because there isn't a realistic chance of it being solved. I don't want you to think that we've looked into a bit, seen something we don't like, and backed away. If we had the evidence, we'd go after whoever it was - I'd personally go after whoever it was. I'm just saying, now he's been told it's over, you need to think long and hard about whether you're really helping him."

"I understand." Sandy said. Her heart was racing. She imagined sitting poor Victor down and looking into his watery eyes to break the news that his son's killer had been his wife, Travis' own mother. She shuddered at the thought.

6

"What's got into you, pet?" Bernice asked, a pile of dirty plates balanced high in her hands.

Sandy gazed into the fridge, unsure what she had been looking for.

"You've been standing there nearly five minutes, lass. What's wrong?"

Sandy shook her head to try and shake the fog that seemed to have taken over her ability to think straight.

"I don't know." She said with a nervous laugh. "I'm not sure where my head's at today, sorry."

"Don't apologise." Bernice said as she added the plates to the growing pile by the sink and gave Sandy's arm a squeeze. "Why don't you go up to the books, though? Send Derrick down here for pot washing? He'll be more use than you... no offence."

"None taken." Sandy said with a laugh. She closed the fridge door and washed her hands.

The cafe was quiet, in the middle of the lull between normal breakfast hours and the start of the lunch rush. Only Dorie Slaughter occupied a table, a mug of tea in front of her as she stared off into space. Sandy remembered her support for Victor Dent. If anyone had information on Valerie, it would be Dorie.

"Morning Dorie." Sandy said, causing the woman to blink her way out of her daydream. "How are you?"

"Not good." Dorie admitted. She cracked her knuckles and winced. "There's trouble in paradise."

Sandy furrowed her brow. "What do you mean?"

"Elaine and my Jim. I dread to say it, you know I don't like gossip Sandy, but I think the novelty's worn off."

"What?" Sandy asked. Dorie's son Jim had seemed well settled with his partner Elaine, who had allowed not only Jim to move in to her cottage but also bring Dorie with him. "You're kidding? They seem so happy."

"Well, my Jim's avoiding her. I mean, I feel for her, but I can't say I'm surprised. She doesn't even know how to make a bread sauce! I mean, how can you expect a man to stay when you're so lacking?"

"I don't think that's what men are looking for nowadays, Dorie."

Dorie rolled her eyes. "Men don't know what they're looking for. They think it's all about looks but then they settle down and they realise they need good dinners to keep 'em going. Elaine's practically forgot where the oven is."

"Has she still got you all on that health kick?" Sandy asked.

"Well, she's trying." Dorie said. "A man can't survive on salad. It's no wonder things are going pear-shaped. Back in my day, a dinner was meat, potatoes and a vegetable. Two vegetables if you were middle-class. That's what a dinner's meant to be."

Sandy smiled. "I remember those dinners."

"These youngsters think they know best with their pasta

and curry but there's nothing wrong with a cooked dinner. I think it's too late for Elaine to learn, though."

"Your Jim doesn't seem like the kind of man who'd go off her for not cooking the right things..." Sandy said, cautiously. Dorie had a complicated love hate relationship with Elaine. On the one hand, Elaine was her son's choice and so must be special because Jim thought so, and on the other hand Elaine was Dorie's strongest competition for her son's attention. That made her the enemy in some ways.

"Well he isn't. He's not fickle, but there's only so much a man can take, Sandy. He's been avoiding her all week - her, not just her cooking. She did a roast chicken last night, I think she knows she's in trouble so she finally listened to me and made a real dinner. He didn't come home. Made up some excuse but I know when my Jim's lying."

"That doesn't sound like Jim." Sandy admitted.

"Hmm." Dorie murmured. She took a swig of her tea.

"Could I pick your brains about something, Dorie? It might distract you from your worries?"

Dorie let out a sigh. "I can't get a minute's peace. Go on then. Quickly."

Sandy smiled to herself. "I wondered what you know about Victor Dent's ex-wife?"

"Well, I know she's still his wife."

"Oh, sorry, I wasn't sure." Sandy apologised.

"As far as I know, there's never been a divorce. There couldn't be really, could there? She disappeared. And he wasn't going out his way to find her."

"It's so sad how they fell apart after losing Travis." Sandy said. She took a seat at the table with Dorie just as Bernice appeared from the kitchen. She eyed the two of them for a moment but said nothing, just rearranged the cakes displayed by the till and took an empty plate back into the kitchen.

"Not surprising."

"No, I bet it often happens."

"I mean, not surprising that it happened to them." Dorie said.

"Did you know them well?"

"I like to make it my business to know everyone well." Dorie said. "Someone has to keep eyes and ears out on village life."

"So what was Valerie like?"

"Before or after?" Dorie asked. "There's a difference."

"Well, both I guess."

"She was fun before. A little bit unpredictable. She kept Victor on his toes. And she was a looker. Nobody really understood why she'd took up with a farmer, with her looks. But they were happy enough. You saw more of her than him, in the village. He was busy with the farm. She'd come down and do the shopping, say hello. Friendly enough. There was a bit of a wild side to her. She'd pick a grape in the shop and taste it and only buy the bunch if it tasted sweet. The times the grocer'd tell her off for that, tell her it was thieving. She weren't bothered."

"She sounds like a character." Sandy said with a smile.

"She had to be. Victor needed someone like that. She gave as good as she got in the arguments, too. They both had a temper." Dorie let out a small laugh. "You'd hear 'em screaming at each other sometimes if you went out walking near the farm. Always made up though, they'd have forgot it an hour later."

"And she changed after?"

"Ohhh." Dorie said. She shook her head. "It happened straight away. Like a switch had been changed in her. We wondered if she'd always had a bit of the madness. You know, the grapes and stuff, it didn't seem that fun when you looked back at it. We all wondered if we should have realised. Or if it came from nowhere."

"What do you mean by madness?"

"She was devastated. Crying all the time, or not crying at all. Completely unpredictable. You'd see her wandering the village in her nightie at all hours. Victor'd come out looking for her. Frantic he was. She'd just look at him like she didn't even know who he was. Tragic, really."

"Surely that's not surprising, though, after what happened?"

"Well, it happens to lots of us Sandy."

"Hmm." Sandy murmured. She hadn't been blessed with children, but still she couldn't begin to imagine how devastating it must be to lose a child. No wonder Valerie had reacted in such a way.

"I know it's not madness, you know." Dorie said. "We know more now, but back then we just thought it was odd. And it was so sad. I'd looked up to her, to be honest, envied her a bit. I'd lost my husband and there she was, living in that big farmhouse, always wearing the latest fashions. She made them herself, you know. Seemed like she'd got it pretty easy."

"And then Travis died."

Dorie almost spat out her tea. "What?"

"And then Travis died? And it all fell apart?"

"No!" Dorie exclaimed.

"But you said it was split into before and after."

"Well, it is. But not before and after he died. It's before and after he was born."

A shiver ran down Sandy's spine at Dorie's words, at the level of her own misunderstanding.

"Everything changed when that boy was born." Dorie said. She wiped the corner of her mouth with a napkin. "Some people said it was because it was a full moon."

Sandy widened her eyes.

"I don't buy that rubbish." Dorie said. "You can't blame the poor boy for being born, that's not right, but he was a handful. He kept them two busy, and she wasn't in her right mind. It all fell to Victor. I think you'd say now that she'd not bonded, I think that's what I've seen them say on TV."

"I've heard that." Sandy said, although her knowledge of babies was slim. "Did she get any help?"

"There wasn't any help, that's what I'm saying. Victor ran the farm and then came home to a baba with a soppin' nappy. Valerie let herself go. I don't think she even got dressed for the first year or two. She always kept her hair neat. Any time you saw her, she'd be combing her hair. Imagine that? A baba with a soppin' nappy and a mother with fresh-combed hair. Not right at all. But we didn't understand, Sandy, back then."

"The poor woman." Sandy whispered.

"It's not just the poor woman. That boy, Travis, he grew to be a menace. A lad can't grow up proper without a mum. No offence, Sandy."

Sandy blinked, realised Dorie was referring to Sandy's mum's death. Sandy herself had been left without a mum at too young an age. She knew that Dorie was right. No child should go through that.

"Victor talks about Travis as if he was an angel." Sandy said, puzzled.

"Course he does." Dorie said. "Victor could never see any bad in the lad, and time has a way of shifting your memories. He was a lovely kid, don't get me wrong, but the devil was in him. He had too much time on his own, time when Valerie should have been raising him."

"What kind of trouble did he get into?"

Dorie shrugged. "It's going back such a long time. It was normal kid stuff, I reckon. He'd bunk off school, I know that much. You'd see the teacher walking through the fields calling his name some days. I remember I found him once, hiding by a hedge, just sitting there. This was a weekend because I was on my way back from the old butcher's and I went there on a Saturday. He was just sat on his own, and I was suspicious straight away because why would a kid be sat on his own on a Saturday? I asked him where his friends were and he said he'd not got any. Not the right way for a boy to grow up, is it?"

Sandy grimaced. "Dorie, do you have any ideas about what happened to Travis?"

The woman shook her head, a little too fast. "I know the rumours."

"Rumours about...?"

"About Valerie. I guess that's why you're asking about her."

Sandy smiled. No wonder DC Sullivan had told her so much; it was all public speculation. She'd thought the officer had been sharing inside information, he was just filling her in on the same gossip that Dorie could have done.

"Do you think it's true?"

"Could be." Dorie admitted. "She wasn't in her right mind, that's all I'll say."

"What happened after he died?"

"To Valerie? It was like a calm came over her. She was herself again. Not exactly the same, but all those demons in her head, they went. She found God. I was pleased for her. She needed something, something to make her more stable.

Victor, well, he got angrier and angrier. And before, she'd argue as good as he would, but after they lost Travis, she wasn't like that any more. He'd shout at her, like he always had, and she'd quote Scripture back at him." Dorie said. She let out a soft chuckle.

"Isn't it a bit weird that she reacted that way? That Travis' death made her more calm?"

Dorie shrugged. "The mind can do strange things to a person, Sandy. And everyone affected by grief has to walk their own path with it."

"That's so true." Sandy said. Dorie looked tired, she noticed. Maybe she was more concerned about the apparent problems in Jim's relationship than she would admit. Sandy gave her hand a squeeze and stood up. "Well, thanks for talking to me. I need to get back to work. Do you need another drink?"

"Not just yet." Dorie said with a smile. Her red lipstick followed the shape of her lips in a shaky line, and Sandy had to look away.

She said goodbye to Dorie and made her way upstairs, where Derrick sat behind the bookshop till pricing up new stock. He grinned when he saw Sandy.

"Come to rescue me, lady?" He asked, already up off his seat. Sandy had never known someone so keen to wash pots. The book store was her sanctuary, but it was too quiet, too sedentary for Derrick's boundless energy.

"Go on, Bernice has got a pile of dishes down there for you." Sandy said with a laugh.

He did a mock salute. "Yes, boss."

He was gone instantly, taking the stairs two or three at a time. She heard his stomping until he reached the ground floor, and could picture him rolling up his sleeves and getting stuck into the washing up.

She breathed a sigh of relief at being in the book store, where there were no less jobs to do, but where the pace was a little slower. Derrick had been partway through inputting a huge box of new stock into the computer system. Sandy had picked up the books herself from a house clearance a few towns away. The collection had belonged to a retired music teacher who was selling up and moving into a care home. His book shelves were full of books on every subject apart from music, which Sandy had found curious.

"Why no music books?" She'd asked the elderly man, whose daughter watched from nearby to make sure his weight was being supported by the walking frame.

He had laughed at her question. "Some things you don't need to learn because they're in your blood. You can feel them, not think them. Like loving a baby."

Sandy remembered the old man's words, and pictured Valerie Dent, lost in a fog of being unable to love her own baby.

What happens, she wonders, when a person can't feel the very thing the world tells them is natural and automatic?

7

*S*andy couldn't remember the last time she had felt so relieved to see her little cottage appear into view. She paused for a moment as a teenager drove by in a neon orange Subaru, everything from the interior apart from the driving seat removed. He revved the engine and stuck his tongue out at her from under his baseball cap, and then he was gone.

She was tempted to give him a two-fingered salute but resisted, her mind taken up with bigger concerns. Had Travis been that kind of menace? A kid desperate to show off his independence?

She shook the thought from her head and crossed the road.

The Cat gazed at her from the living room window, and Sandy grinned.

"Evening, Sandy." Jim Slaughter called. Since he and Dorie had moved in with Elaine, they had become Sandy's neighbours. They - or, in particular, Dorie - were quieter than Sandy might have expected. She'd never expected Jim to be anything other than the takeaway-food addict he had lived up to being. She could tell which evenings Jim and Elaine were out as the television played endlessly all evening at a ridiculous volume, broadcasting programmes that Sandy guessed to be soap operas. Causing any sound to pass through the thick cottage walls was quite the achievement, and Sandy smiled to herself whenever it happened. There were worse noises to hear coming from a neighbour, she knew.

"Jim, how are you?" Sandy asked. Their cottages were separated by a low hedge, and Jim approached his side and gestured for her to move closer. He was dressed in a pale blue t-shirt that was slightly too short. It revealed the swell of his stomach and a patch of dark hair escaping from the waistband of his jeans in a line towards his belly button. The sight was strangely intimate. She averted her eyes.

"Lovely evening." He said, and she nodded. Elaine's car wasn't on the driveway.

"Everything ok?" She asked again.

He looked down at the ground and nodded and the motion made his last chin bounce on and off of his neck.

"I'm putting the kettle on if you want to pop in for a drink?" Sandy suggested.

Jim grinned. "Got any biscuits?"

"I might have a few custard creams left in the barrel." Sandy admitted. She occasionally bought a selection pack of biscuits from the discount shop in the next village, and while she would greedily make her way through the bourbons and the digestives, the custard creams gathered dust in the barrel. It seemed that her regular visitors shared her dislike of them. But, if Elaine's health regime was as bad as Dorie said, Sandy suspected that Jim would welcome any biscuits she could offer.

She unlocked the front door and dropped her bag to the

floor, then kicked off her shoes. If Jim wasn't popping in, she'd have headed straight up to her bedroom to get changed into her pyjamas. The proximity of the thought of her getting undressed to her noticing Jim's snail trail of hair made her cringe. She hoped he didn't think she was making a pass at him.

Too late to do anything other than host her neighbour as offered, she walked down the hallway and clicked the kettle on.

Jim appeared in the doorway, oversized and uncomfortable.

"Come in, make yourself at home." Sandy called. "We're neighbours now."

"Well, yeah." Jim said with a nervous smile. "It feels strange walking in someone's house and it not being police business."

"How *is* work?" Sandy asked. Safe territory, work and the weather. Being British gave a person satisfying conversational boundaries.

He shrugged. "Same old, really."

"You know DC Sullivan's been back in town?"

Jim did a double take, eyebrows furrowed. "Really?"

She nodded. "He's closed the investigation into Travis Dent's death."

Jim looked blank for a moment, then his mouth formed a small circle. "Ohhh, Victor's son? I wonder why he's done that now."

It was a good question, and one Sandy hadn't considered.

What had made the police close the case at that particular time? And why had DC Sullivan thought it so urgent that he had to be at Victor's farm at the crack of dawn to share the news?

"I don't know." Sandy said. "The whole thing just doesn't seem right."

She passed Jim a strong mug of tea, three sugars, and lead him into the living room, where he dropped his weight into the chair furthest from the window.

"Did you say you had biscuits?" Jim asked.

She laughed and returned to the kitchen, fetched the almost-empty barrel, and placed it in front of him on the coffee table. She wasn't sure whether to be relieved or offended that Jim's interest in her clearly extended only to the contents of her biscuit barrel.

"Thanks." He said. He took out a custard cream, screwed his nose up in disappointment, but dunked it in his tea nonetheless.

"Do you know much about the case? About Travis?" Sandy asked. She took a sip of her mocha and sat back in her chair.

"Me?" Jim asked, mouth full of custard cream. "Nah."

"You haven't heard any rumours or anything?" Sandy pushed.

He shrugged. "I don't really hear much. I like to keep my head down."

Sandy nodded, disappointed. "People seem to think his mum's the prime suspect."

"Prime suspect of what? They never said it was murder, did they? They dragged him out the river."

"Well, no." Sandy admitted. "But some people think it was suspicious."

"Oh." Jim said. "Must be tough for Victor, not knowing what happened."

"Exactly."

"You're looking into it, aren't you?"

"Is it that obvious?" Sandy asked with a smile. "I need to work on my investigative skills."

"Well, you just need to be careful." Jim warned.

"Careful?"

"Things are never really what you expect they are." Jim said. He gazed out of the window as a car went past. Sandy turned and saw Elaine pull on to her driveway.

"Is everything okay, Jim?"

"Big changes are coming." Jim said with a distracted smile.

"Good changes, I hope?"

"We'll see." He said. He took a greedy swig of his tea.

"Elaine's home." Sandy said. "Not that I'm trying to rush you off."

"Oh, I'm going out." Jim said.

Sandy's heart sank. Dorie had been telling the truth. He *was* avoiding Elaine.

"Anywhere nice?"

"Not really, no." He said. "I've been doing some overtime, there's this big drive to get all the files in order, check evidence and things on the live cases. I'm pulling a few night shifts."

"Night shifts? In Waterfell Tweed?" Sandy asked in disbelief.

"Oh no, over in the city. They didn't have enough volunteers for the shifts so they put word out over here."

"Well, keeps you out of trouble, I guess." Sandy said.

"Nice easy work." Jim said. "And I get to go in my own clothes. Put the radio on. There's worse ways to spend a night. Money'll come in handy too."

"Well, rather you than me." Sandy said. "I like my sleep too much."

Jim finished his tea and a stern look crossed his face. "I wasn't sleeping anyway. Might as well be out earning."

"Makes sense." She said. His repeated mention of money made her insides churn. His living expenses were only going to increase if he was thinking of moving out, of leaving Elaine.

"Right, thanks for the tea Sandy. I hope the biscuit can remain our secret."

"It absolutely can." Sandy agreed. She showed Jim to the door and watched as he walked furtively back across to his own cottage and climbed into his car, without so much as a hello or goodbye to Elaine.

8

*T*he village library had three computers available to use for an hour at a time.

Sandy had scanned her library card and booked herself a session after twenty minutes of connecting and disconnecting her modem at home. The internet had always been unreliable in the cottage, but Sandy made do. She didn't need to go online much, anyway. Time spent on social media was time away from reading.

The library computer was historic, the screen small but the monitor itself cavernous in its depth.

The librarian had warned her that any printing, even accidental printing, cost 10p per sheet, and that mucky websites were blocked. Sandy had felt herself blush at the second warning, even though she had no intentions of trying to find anything at all mucky.

Apart from her and the draconian librarian, the library was empty. It broke Sandy's heart to see what could be such a vital part of village life be such a wasted opportunity. The bizarre and restrictive opening hours didn't help. Nobody in the village seemed to know when the library was open, and the librarian seemed personally affronted whenever anyone suggested that a sign publicising the opening times should be pinned up somewhere.

Sandy heard the distantly-familiar wake up noise of Windows 95 and waited three minutes for the machine to fully power up. Internet Explorer was the only browser the machine could handle, and Sandy clicked the icon for it with relish. It was like stepping back in time.

In the search bar, she typed in Travis' name.

The first result, which loaded after a full minute's wait, was a report of a press conference held after his body had been found.

Travis Dent, 26, was described as being a perfect son by his parents, Victor and Valerie. The couple spoke in a press conference, where they asked anyone with information to come forward.

"Awful business." The librarian, Enid, said. She hovered behind Sandy's chair, glasses hanging from a string around her neck, bosom sitting atop her elasticated skirt, cheeks ruddy from a middle-class drinking habit.

"It's so sad." Sandy agreed. She didn't like being watched but she was ready to listen to anyone who might know something.

"You know why they do that, don't you?"

"Do what?"

"Make the parents ask for information?"

"Because it's more powerful than the police doing it?" Sandy guessed.

"Nah." Enid said. "It's when they think the parents are guilty. They've got a room full of psychologists watching everything the parents say, how they act, what they don't do. They catch plenty a killer that way."

A chill ran through Sandy's body and she shivered involuntarily.

"He'd got a temper, that farmer. Still has."

"Victor?"

Enid nodded. "Why you looking at this, anyway? It's old news."

"The police have just decided to close the case. I was just curious about it."

"Ah, yeah, should've guessed. They'll be doing that on a few cases I reckon."

"Why?"

"Well, it's this national review. Don't you watch the news?'"

Sandy felt her cheeks burn. "I haven't had much chance."

"Well, there's a big police enquiry going on. The top dogs think cases haven't been handled properly. All live cases, no matter how old, are being reviewed. Imagine the work that's going to involve?"

Sandy thought back to Jim, his confidence that his night work was easy. It didn't seem like he realised the magnitude of the review that was needed.

"So the more cases the police close, the less work they have to do."

"And the more time they can spend catching criminals now, let's be honest. They shouldn't be focusing their attention on things this old. It makes no sense."

"So, this review? When did it start?"

"Ooh, you'll have to watch the news for the details. There was a cut off, might have been Thursday. It was nine in the morning, I know that. As if the police work 9 til 5."

"Thursday?" Sandy repeated. The morning she had

received the frantic call from Victor, right before the 9am deadline for the police to close as many files as they could.

Sandy felt her heartbeat race. Travis' file hadn't been closed because too much time had passed. It had been closed because someone higher up, over DC Sullivan's head, wanted to make sure no more time was spent reviewing it.

A man dead.

A family without answers.

And it came down to not wanting to invest the time needed.

**

Sandy barged her way out of the library, her lips set tight.

The village square was quiet. Another big football match was in progress. She could hear the steady roar from The Tweed. Everyone became a football fan and an expert when the national team played.

Ahead of her, tucked into a doorway, she spotted Bomber and waved at him. He didn't see her, his vision blocked by the lamppost between them.

She watched as Gus Sanders, the butcher, approached him and moved into the doorway with him.

She watched as Bomber got right into Gus' face, his eyes angry and his arms gesticulating wildly.

And she watched as Gus pushed him away and stormed out from the doorway and into the pub.

"Bomber?" She called. Bomber looked up at her, his leather jacket hanging off one shoulder from the power behind Gus' shove.

"Hey, Sand." He said.

"What was that about?"

"Oh, nothing." Bomber said with an eye roll. "Just another drunk who doesn't like being told to slow it down."

"I thought you didn't know him?"

"I know his sort." Bomber said. He turned to the pub, but Gus was already out of sight.

"He's a local lad, you two might have known each other when you were..."

"No." Bomber said. "Tom's told me his name. I didn't know him."

"Okay." Sandy said, unsure why the subject seemed to have touched such a raw nerve. "He's been doing really well lately, with the drinking. I don't know what's happened."

'Well, I don't care." Bomber said.

Sandy frowned. He could be all kinds of things, but he wasn't mean-spirited.

"You can't trust a drunk." Bomber said. "I can't forget that for a minute in this line of work."

"Drinkers are hardly your enemy, Bomber." Sandy said. "They're the reason you have a job. You and Tom."

He gave her a short nod and adjusted the jacket. "There's drinkers, and drunks."

And with that, he stormed back towards the pub.

**

Sandy followed out of curiosity.

The pub was crowded, people standing inches apart, invading personal boundaries as they all gazed at the big screen. The atmosphere was good-natured, with groups of young men standing with arms around each other. Even the couples were fixated on the TV.

Sandy searched the bar until her gaze fell on Gus, who sat alone at the bar, an amber pint in front of him, his head drooped. She thought he was asleep for a moment, until he lifted the glass and took a drink.

Bomber was behind the bar, and Tanya and Tom stood by his side. Full staffing. The football was good for business.

Tom looked across and saw her, and his face lit up in the way it did every time he noticed her. Her stomach flipped. She wondered if, or when, she would stop having that effect on him.

"Could I steal you away?" She asked.

"You'll be okay for ten minutes, won't you?" Tom asked Bomber, who nodded, still tense.

Tom led her by the hand around the back of the bar, and through the door into the private living area. Up the stairs, he took her into her favourite room, the library. It had been such a surprise when he had shown it to her for the first time, and the novelty hadn't worn off.

"I miss you." He said.

"Oh, I miss you too." Sandy said. She kissed him on the forehead. He still looked a little off colour. "Are you getting enough rest?"

He nodded. Sandy had ordered that until he was better, he should work reduced hours and not spend his free time with her. He needed to sleep.

"I slept fourteen hours last night." He admitted with a coy smile. "It was like being a teenager again."

"That's brilliant. Your body obviously needs it."

Tom nodded and broke into a huge yawn. He covered his mouth and she laughed.

"I'm looking forward to spending some more time with you, though."

"I know." Sandy said. "But there's no rush, we've got the rest of our lives."

It was meant to be a flippant comment, but the gravity of her words hit her as soon as she finished talking.

Tom met her gaze, dark eyes serious. "Yes we have."

Her heart flipped with relief. It seemed there was nothing she could do to scare the man away.

"Can I ask you something?"

"If you're going to test me on the novel you let me borrow, I wouldn't bother. I haven't stayed awake long enough to get past page four."

Sandy laughed. She'd given him a cozy mystery novel to help pass his down time. Something light and entertaining was just what he needed while he felt so awful. "It's not that. Although you will enjoy that book when you get to it, I promise. But, no... it's erm, is anything going on with Poppy and Gus?"

"Not that I know of, what do you mean?" Tom asked. Poppy was his sister, and Gus' long-suffering wife.

"I just feel like Gus is going down hill again." Sandy said. It was difficult, saying such a thing about his brother-in-law.

"Drinking?" Tom asked. "Yeah, he's definitely drinking more."

"Do you have to serve him?" She asked.

"No, but it's best if we do." Tom said. "He's safe here. We can keep an eye on him, tell him to slow down when he needs to. If he knows he won't get served, he'll go somewhere else, where they won't care about him like we do."

"I saw him in a bit of a heated talk with Bomber earlier." Sandy said. "It's weird, to say they don't know each other."

"Oh, they know each other."

"What do you mean?"

"First time Gus saw Bomber was back, it was like he'd seen a ghost."

"Bomber's told me they don't know each other."

"Weird." Tom said, with a shrug. He yawned again.

"I'm sorry. You need to get some rest. I just wanted to talk to you about Gus. You don't think he's having problems at home or something?"

Tom shook his head. "Poppy's put up with years of this. Why would there be problems now?"

"Yeah, I guess."

"Look, I'll keep an eye on him, okay?" Tom said.

She smiled and kissed his forehead again. "Why don't you get to bed? I'll tell Bomber."

"I think I might." He said, eyelids heavy. "I'm sorry, Sand. When I'm better, let's go away? Just me and you?"

"That sounds perfect." She said. "If I can get some answers for Victor, I'll be ready for a break."

9

*S*andy parked her old Land Rover near Black Rock and sat inside for a moment as the engine idled.

Coral sat beside her in the passenger seat, swiping endlessly.

"Found him yet?" Sandy asked. Coral hadn't made a word of conversation since they'd left the cafe together at the end of the work day.

"Hmm?" Coral asked. She noticed they had arrived at their destination and finally planted the phone in her tiny handbag.

"Mr Perfect?"

"Ha ha." Coral said with an eye roll. "I'm sure he's not going to be hanging around waiting for me to swipe on his face."

"Well, he might be walking right past you. You won't notice with your head in your phone like that."

"You're tetchy. What's up?" Coral asked. She peered at her sister through new, oversized glasses that made her look more like the journalist she used to be than the waitress she was.

"We just drove this whole way and you didn't even ask me how I am."

"Oh… well, how are you?"

Sandy sighed. "It's too late now. And I'm fine. But your face is always in that damn phone. I'd just like to have some time with my sister, if that's not too much to ask."

Coral shrugged, her eyes wide with confusion. She'd always been the same, since she got her first job in a newsroom and decided that she needed to be connected at all times. She paid for some kind of magic box that made her own Internet at home lightning fast, as if a slight disruption in the constant stream of incoming information would be disastrous. Although, recently, her online activity was more about searching for the ideal man than the juiciest news story.

Sandy quite liked the thought that there were times when she was unreachable. The idea of getting home, locking her front door and turning her phone off. The world was overwhelming at times. It was nice to forget about it all at times.

Not that she'd been able to do that since Victor's phone call a few days ago.

Travis Dent, a man she'd never met, had taken over her every waking thought and most of her dreams.

Her stomach churned as she stared out at the farmhouse, sat among barren farmland, its successful days gone to ruin.

"Are we going in, then?" Coral interjected.

"I guess we'd better." Sandy said. She unbuckled her seat belt and opened the door, the rickety vehicle creaking with her every movement. She'd have to replace the car at some point and when the day came, she planned to buy another old Land Rover. She liked driving something with personality and this car, with the gear stick that treated gear changes like an arm wrestling competition, had plenty of that.

Coral trudged ahead towards the farmhouse, stomping through the long grass while Sandy stuck to the route that had been flattened by footfall. Coral stopped at the door, though, and turned to wait for Sandy to join her.

Sandy knocked, the noise echoing across the empty fields. The quiet was eerie.

Victor appeared after a few moments, freshly shaved, dressed in a yellow shirt that may have originally been white. A flat cap sat on his head.

A strangled cry escaped him as he saw Sandy, and her chest constricted.

She had become the visitor to dread.

A woman who could only bring bad news, whether she brought news or not.

He held the door open and she entered, Coral falling into step behind her.

"This is my sister, Victor. Her name's Coral." Sandy explained as they sat in the living room. Victor took his usual seat and turned the football highlights off the TV.

"Nice to meet you." Coral said with a polite smile. She looked like a journalist sat there, legs together, arms clasped in her lap. All that was missing was her notebook, and Sandy knew she still carried one in her handbag out of habit.

"Huh." Victor said with a nod, as if the words were a surprise. A pleasantry he didn't hear. As they must be. "So, let's not mess around. You found anything?"

"Possibly." Sandy said. She took a deep breath. "I know why they closed the case. There's a national enquiry into all historic cases, over concerns that they weren't looked into properly. Apparently, police departments were trying to sign off as many cold cases as they could before 9 o'clock Thursday morning."

"Is that right." He said, but he seemed less surprised by this news than Coral's suggestion that she was pleased to meet him.

"They're trying to save resources, like we thought..." Sandy began.

"Or they're hiding something." Coral said, out of nowhere. Sandy looked at her, her brows furrowed. Coral had offered to visit Victor with her because she had no other plans for the night. She'd never mentioned that she had her own ideas to discuss.

"Hiding something?"

"You see this a lot. Whenever there's a review like this, it's time to check through the records and see what skeletons you need to hide." She explained. Well, that explained the posture. She really was in journalist mode.

"What skeletons could there be?"

"Oh, plenty." She said. "And not necessarily anything ominous. But, mistakes were made back then. And with DCI Simmons, who really knows what was happening."

"Simmons was an ignorant pig." Victor said. "And he's never changed. He should have come and given us the news about closing the case."

"He's retired." Sandy explained.

"Well, he's gone. I wouldn't call it retired." Coral said.

Sandy shot her sister a look. Why hadn't she mentioned any of this earlier?

"I always said he were dirty." Victor said.

"What's the deal with him?" Sandy asked.

"There were lots of stories about him. Stories about people buying the result they wanted... bribes, you know."

"But how could -"

"Evidence went missing, quite a lot." Coral said with a shrug. "And maybe evidence was planted too, it's harder to prove that. It reached the point where they couldn't keep dodging the questions any longer, so he was retired."

"So you're saying my son's case has been closed to cover up for a dirty cop?" Victor asked.

"It's a possibility." Coral said.

"Maybe I should go and talk to Simmons." Sandy said. "Ask him what he remembers, suss him out."

"I doubt you'd get far. He's moved away."

"So he was a local?" Sandy asked.

"Oh yeah, the Simmons family were here for generations." Coral said.

Victor sat quietly in his chair. It was impossible to read whether he was taking in the conversation.

"I thought the police cared." Victor said, his voice low and dangerous. "I thought they were there to help, to catch the bad guys and lock 'um away."

"I think most of them are, Victor." Sandy said, but her thoughts flashed to Jim Slaughter, who while harmless wasn't particularly helpful either. She'd been brought up believing the same things as Victor, that the police were there to protect and serve, to investigate and find justice. But it was her, not a police officer, who was sat in Victor's house trying to solve his son's murder.

"So, that's it then? Case closed?" Victor asked.

Sandy shifted in the seat. "Not quite."

Victor looked up, hopeful enough to break a heart.

"It's nothing concrete. And it's not easy for me to say."

"Just spit it out." He commanded.

She took a breath. Coral nodded at her to speak. "The

most common theory, and this is among the police, is that Valerie did it."

"Val... Val did it?" Victor said. He blinked, open-mouthed. "Did what?"

"Killed him. They think she was ill, Victor, not well mentally."

"Well, she weren't, but no, no, no. She didn't hurt him. He was her boy!"

"People say she didn't really bond with him, when he was born."

"She didn't. She never did. But plenty of women struggle after having a babba. She didn't hurt him."

"Do you know that, Victor? Or do you really want to believe it?"

"I know it." He said, voice barely audible. He looked down. "I remember everything about that night. That night when he didn't come home."

"Were you with her? Is that how you can be so sure?"

"No, I weren't with her." He admitted. "I weren't with her much at all by that time. We were falling apart. She had a caravan, out there." He gestured towards the back of the house absentmindedly. "It were falling apart as much as we were, but she loved it out there. It were like she needed to escape, needed to forget about us. She were living out there more than in here. I remember that night, I stood in the kitchen making a brew after putting the laundry in, she didn't do owt like that. I stood and I watched. I could see her, see the shape of her out there in the caravan. She'd got some music on I reckon, she were dancing. Maybe the music was in her head. And I watched her, and I thought maybe I should walk across there, offer her a brew, and dance with her. She was so close, but she was miles away. I knew I couldn't reach her. So I didn't try. I just stood there and watched her. She danced until her feet were red raw, and I stood and watched her."

Sandy watched him and tried to smile but the weight of her mouth was too heavy to move. She tried to picture him, as a younger man; a father, a farmer, a husband who feared losing his wife and had no clue he was about to lose his son.

"Okay, well that answers that point." Sandy said. "I'll keep investigating."

"Do you reckon it's hopeless?" Victor asked. His voice broke on the question, betraying its importance.

"I don't think it's hopeless Victor, but I do worry. I worry that no matter what the answer turns out to be, it might make things worse."

He let out a small, bitter laugh. "Things can't get any worse, lass. Trust me on that."

10

*S*andy measured out the flour, salt, baking powder and caster sugar, then mixed warm milk and eggs in another bowl. She added the wet mixture little by little to the dry mix, stirring to create a batter. And then, she added a teaspoon of vanilla essence.

It was her mum's recipe. No matter how tight money was, and there was often too much month left at the end of the money, she always made sure they had these ingredients in. And while their cupboards were stacked with the blue and white value options of most items, the vanilla essence was bought from a little independent baking shop in the village square. They could have bought a whole sack of potatoes and a small joint of meat for the same price as the vanilla essence cost, but it was an argument her father knew not to have.

Sandy continued to stir the mix long after it had reached the perfect consistency, enjoying the hypnotic process of the wooden spoon cutting through the batter.

"Ooh, what's this then?" Bernice asked as she appeared in the kitchen.

"I bought a waffle maker." Sandy said with a smile.

"Excellent!" Bernice said. "I love a waffle. Have we got berries?"

Sandy nodded. "I'm going to cut some strawberries up next. Do you want to write it on the specials board?"

"I'd rather just keep it for me, to be honest, but go on then." Bernice said with a laugh. She disappeared back out to the cafe and Sandy covered the mixing bowl with cling-film and placed it in the fridge.

The waffle maker had been on sale when she did her own food shopping the night before, and she'd bought it on a whim, her mind full of childhood memories. Weekend waffles had been one of the great joys of her childhood. Her mum had bought their waffle maker after their trip to America, where they had seen one in action for the first time and declared it to be the greatest invention in the world.

Waffles were on the menu every weekend after that.

Well, until her mum had died. Nobody touched the waffle maker then.

"You've got your first order." Bernice called, disturbing her thoughts.

"Dorie?" Sandy guessed. Dorie Slaughter was the cafe's most loyal customer. She always had been, but with Elaine's strict health regime at home, Dorie had never eaten so many meals at Books and Bakes.

"It's Elaine, actually."

"Elaine? Eating waffles?"

"Why? They're vegetarian, aren't they?"

"Well, yeah, I thought she was eating healthy, though."

Bernice shrugged. She stayed firmly out of all village gossip.

Sandy clicked the power outlet on and waited for the

machine to heat up, then poured two generous scoops of batter into the waffle maker, closed it to, and set the timer for seven minutes. Four minutes made pale, anaemic waffles. Seven minutes made perfectly brown waffles that just begged to be eaten.

She chopped strawberries into halves until the waffle maker beeped to announce that seven minutes had passed. The mound of juicy red strawberries should be enough for the day's waffle orders. She popped one into her mouth - delicious.

She flipped the waffle onto a plate, sliced it into quarters, topped it with a generous portion of strawberries and drizzled a little maple syrup over it.

"Looks amazing. Save me a portion for lunch, eh pet?" Bernice asked.

Sandy grinned.

She was determined to forget about the heavy burden resting on her shoulders and focus on the cafe for the day. She would make delicious food and serve it to people. She'd rescue Coral, who still couldn't make a cappuccino, and she'd chat with the villagers who kept her in business with their frequent visits and orders.

The simplicity of the day's plans made a deep peace come over her as she carried the food out and placed it in front of Elaine, who wore more make-up than normal and stared at her phone, face-up, on the table in front of her.

"Ooh, thanks Sandy, this looks lovely."

"It must be something special to tempt you!" Sandy joked. Elaine looked at her blankly. "Well, you know, with your health kick."

"Health kick?"

"You're all trying to be good aren't you, at yours?" Sandy asked.

"Not really." Elaine said. "Is that what they're saying?"

Sandy felt her cheeks flush. She shouldn't have said anything. So much for an uncomplicated day.

"I've probably got the wrong end of the stick." Sandy said. "You know, I've always got half an ear on a conversation. Anyway, enjoy!"

"Sandy, wait?" Elaine said. Sandy's heart sank. "Have you got a minute?"

"Erm, a minute, sure." Sandy said. She took a seat next to Elaine as the doorbell rang out. Poppy Sanders walked in and placed a takeaway drink order at the counter. Coral nodded as she rung it through the till, but eyed Sandy in panic.

"What have they been saying, about the health kick?"

"Oh, honestly, Elaine, I don't know."

Elaine sighed. "I don't cook much, but it's not that I'm starving anyone. I mean, they're both grown ups, they can find the kitchen themselves, you know?"

"Well, absolutely." Sandy said.

"Jim's so traditional, I think he expected dinner to be on the table for him every night. I worry I'm a disappointment to him."

Sandy felt her cheeks flush as her mind flashed back to her conversation with Dorie. "I'm sure you're not, Elaine. You're lovely. He's a lucky man."

"I made a chicken dinner the other night, but he didn't come home. He's doing so much overtime." She said. "Maybe I should make more of an effort, since he's working so hard. I've been out of the habit for so long, though, I just get in and have a sandwich or something. Some nights I don't have anything at all."

"It must be a huge change." Sandy said. Elaine had lived alone since her husband had died many years before, and then all of a sudden she had not just Jim, but his mother too, living with her. It wasn't a change Sandy would like to have made.

"It's not that bad." Elaine said with a thoughtful smile. "It's nice to have some noise in the house again, to be honest. It's been so quiet for so long."

Sandy smiled. "Well, let me leave you to enjoy your breakfast."

"I've lost my appetite." Elaine said, and she burst into tears. "Oh Sandy, I'm so sorry. I just don't know what to do."

"What's wrong?"

"I think he's got another woman." Elaine said between sobs.

"Who? Jim? No way!"

"I think he has, Sandy." Elaine said. She wiped her eyes and regained composure. "He's acting strange. He's never at home, and he's been ever so secretive. He keeps getting these phone calls, always leaves the house when he has one."

"Elaine... listen, all of that does sound odd when you say it like that. But this is Jim. He's totally smitten with you. Why don't you just ask him what's going on?"

"I can't." She said. "I don't think I want to know. It took me so long to open up to someone again, Sandy. I don't think I can go through losing him. I'll look so daft."

"Of course you wouldn't!" Sandy protested. "Look, if you were right - and I still don't think you are - but if you were, he's the one who would look daft."

"I guess so. But you know how people like to gossip."

"The biggest gossip in this village is Dorie, and she wouldn't be wanting people knowing that about her son."

"That's a good point." Elaine said with a deep sigh. "I'm sorry. I don't know what came over me. You know what, you're right. I've been through worse. If he's had his head turned, I'll get through it."

"Everything okay?" Poppy called across to their table. Coral had managed to serve her.

"Oh yes, yes, thanks for checking Poppy." Elaine said with a smile.

"Tough day coming up?" Sandy asked, gesturing to the caffeine-to-go in Poppy's hand.

"You could say that." Poppy said with a laugh. She was a sing-song voice and a bright green tea dress, a genuinely concerned face. The primary teacher every child must dream of. "Some Mondays just need an extra caffeine hit."

"How's Gus?" Sandy asked.

Poppy's brow twitched at the mention of her husband's name. "He's alright. Actually, we were just saying we should have you and Tom over for dinner."

"Really?" Sandy asked. Poppy and Tom didn't have the kind of relationship where they hosted dinner for each other. In fact, Sandy had only recently realised that they were brother and sister. "That would be nice."

"Come over tonight." Poppy suggested, heading towards the door. "It won't be anything fancy but I reckon I've got some pizzas."

"Okay." Sandy said. She'd already got plans to see Tom that night. "We'll bring the beers."

The words were out of her mouth before she could stop them. Beers. The perfect gift for an alcoholic whose recovery already seemed to be in jeopardy.

"Perfect!" Poppy said with a kind smile. She must have seen the horror written across Sandy's face.

"See what I mean?" Elaine said with a sniff.

"Erm, not really?" Sandy admitted.

"Family. It's all about family."

"Well, things aren't always what they seem." Sandy said. The dinner invitation was unusual. She wondered if there was more to it. Maybe Poppy planned to stage an intervention to get Gus back off the bottle. "Nobody's got the perfect family life, Elaine."

"Oh, I know that." Elaine said with a sad smile as she gazed into the distance. "But for a long time I didn't have any family life. I don't want perfect, I just want to keep what I've got."

"What you've got is Dorie Slaughter under your roof, you're a saint."

"She's alright deep down, really. She just loves Jim so much. I can hardly criticise the woman for that, can I?"

"I guess not, that's what mothers do isn't it." Sandy said.

"Well. Not all of them." Elaine said. "And that makes the good ones even more special, I reckon."

11

"You're kidding." Tom said. He sat in the library in his living quarters, dressed in a pale pink t-shirt and a pair of dark blue corduroy trousers. It was so good to see him back to 100%, Sandy wanted to hold him and never let him go.

"I couldn't really say no." Sandy said, although that wasn't true. She could have said no, but she was too curious.

"Let's cancel?" Tom suggested.

Sandy let out a laugh but he didn't smile. "You're serious?"

He nodded. "The thought of a quiet night with you has been all that's got me through the last few days of being sick as a dog. Come on, let's make up an excuse and stay here."

"We can't do that, Tom."

"Why? Have they hired a chef, or something?"

"Well, no... Poppy said she might have some pizzas." Sandy admitted. Her own faux pas returned to her and she felt herself blush. "And I said I'd take the beers."

"Smooth." Tom said with a grin.

"It's not funny! I'm fairly sure that makes me the worst dinner guest ever."

"Even more reason to cancel, then. In fact, they're probably hoping you do. Poppy probably wishes she'd never invited you."

"Ouch." Sandy teased. "Are you really that desperate for a night with me?"

"Absolutely." He said. "I'd even let you pick a chick flick if we could just have a movie night."

Sandy felt herself pulled between keeping her commitment, and doing what she'd rather do as well. Poppy and Gus were okay, but they weren't her first choice of people to spend an evening with.

"I didn't realise I could say no to an invitation from your sister?"

"Why?" Tom asked. "Is that a thing?"

"I just thought, you know… family loyalty and all that."

"I can't remember the last time I had dinner at hers, we're not that kind of family. You could have said no. Or said you'd check with me. Are you saying you don't really want to go?"

"Well…" Sandy said, then allowed her voice to trail off.

"So let's cancel." Tom said. "They'll understand."

"I can't." She said, the decision clear and made. "I don't like letting people down, it's not nice. I know it's a pain, but let's just go for a quick dinner and then we can leave early and maybe have some time to ourselves?"

Tom sighed and stood up from the chair. He walked across to her, his feet bare and his trousers a little too long, and planted a kiss on her lips. "I love you."

"I love you, too."

"Thanks for doing the right thing." He said with a smile.

**

They had to wait an awkward amount of time for the door to be answered.

They had gone past the amused phase, and the awkward phase, and were approaching the irritated phase when a red-faced Poppy appeared at the door, still in the green tea dress. She forced a smile on to her face.

"Come in!" She sang, louder than was needed. "I'm so sorry, I thought we'd said 8pm."

"Oh, I thought we..." Sandy said, but she couldn't remember who had set the time. "You know, you're probably right. We can come back later if we're too early?"

"Or rearrange?" Tom suggested. Sandy elbowed him.

"No, no, it's only frozen pizzas. They'll only take ten minutes. Come in, come in!" Poppy sang, and something about her voice, her manic appearance, left Sandy unconvinced.

"Where's Gus?" Tom asked as they entered the living room. A beer can had been left on the coffee table. Poppy scooped it up, but not before they'd both noticed it.

"Just freshening himself up, I suppose. You don't want the meat smell on him!"

Sandy gave an awkward smile.

"Drinks?" Poppy offered.

"I'll get a beer." Tom said, then noticed Sandy's glare. "Water, actually. Water."

"Ooh yes, water for me too." Sandy said with an enthusiasm she didn't feel. She began to wish she'd taken Tom up on the offer of cancelling.

Gus walked into the room a few moments after the oven buzzed to announce that the pizzas were ready. The meat smell, as Poppy described it, had been replaced by the ale smell, and he grabbed Sandy in a hug that was uncomfortably tight and lasted longer than she would have liked.

"Well, this is nice." Poppy said as she brought out plates for each of them. Each plate had two slices of Margherita pizza and a meagre selection of pre-packed salad leaves.

"Mm, looks wonderful." Sandy said. She tried to sound sincere, but her business made her something of a food snob. She was particular about the places where she dined and the food she ate. But this was Tom's family. And Tom certainly felt like he was her family, which meant Poppy and Gus were her family too.

"Honestly, Sandy, that supermarket across town, it's got some great offers on." Poppy said as she took her seat. The second she sat down, Gus stood up. Sandy heard him open the can of beer in the kitchen. He took a long sip of it as he walked back into the room.

Sandy and Tom exchanged glances but said nothing.

"Do you like oven chips?" Poppy asked, voice unnaturally high and happy. "Oven chips, 59p. I mean, you see oven chips for a quid, don't ya, but 59p? There's no reason to peel a potato anymore, is there?"

"Well, at those prices, I guess not." Sandy said with a smile. She couldn't remember the last time an oven chip had crossed her mouth or her mind.

"How's school?" Tom asked, steering his sister away from the riveting topic of supermarket shopping.

"Not as exciting as what Sandy's up to." Poppy said with a grin.

Sandy looked at her, mouth full of undercooked pizza. Had Poppy invited her over to get the gossip about Travis Dent?

"Sandy's always up to something." Tom said with a tight

smile. "I'm much better, by the way. Thanks for your sisterly concern."

"Were you ill?" Poppy asked as she stabbed a piece of browned lettuce with her fork.

"He's been doing the dying swan for days in the pub, I told ya that." Gus slurred.

Sandy let out a small cough. "He's still not totally better though, are you Tom?"

She kicked his leg under the table and he shook his head. "I'm tiring easily."

"You talk so much rubbish Gus, I can't always listen to you. What's wrong, Tom? You should have said Sandy, you shouldn't have dragged him out when he's ill."

"You're right." Sandy dead panned. The meal was a disaster. "Are you okay, Tom, or do you need to go home?"

"Let's finish dinner, but then we'll make a move. If that's okay?"

"Of course it is." Poppy sang. She eyed her brother with concern. "It's not like you to get ill. Make sure you look after yourself."

"I'll make sure he does." Sandy said. She laid her cutlery on the table.

"Not hungry?" Poppy asked, noting the amount of untouched food still on her plate.

"No, I'm fine. I'm full." Sandy said, hoping there would be no offer of dessert. She felt quite queasy and hoped she wasn't catching Tom's bug. Or food poisoning from under-cooked pizza.

"What's she up to, then?" Gus asked in between slugs of beer.

"Well." Poppy said. Her cheeks were crimson. "It's not my place to say, really."

"There's an old murder she's looking into, that's all."

Tom said nonchalantly, as if she was considering going to bed an hour later than normal or something as trivial. "But it's proving hard work."

"You need to leave that stuff to the professionals." Gus said.

"Well, I would, but the professionals have closed the case."

"That's it then, surely?" Gus said.

"Not if I have anything to do with it." Sandy said, with steely determination.

"It must be so exciting." Poppy gushed.

"It isn't." Sandy said. "It's frustrating and upsetting. I feel like I've got the whole world on my shoulders and nothing I do is getting me further along, or not quick enough anyway."

"Oh." Poppy said. She offered Sandy a polite smile. She was nice, really, really nice. If Sandy had been blessed with children, she'd want them to have a teacher like Poppy. She just wasn't sure that she wanted a friend like Poppy. The connection wasn't there between them.

"Can we get going?" Tom asked. "I'm going downhill, sorry guys."

"Oh, no, don't apologise." Poppy said, her voice rich with relief.

"I'll see ya tomorrow anyways matey." Gus said with a wink.

"You said you were finishing off those cans tonight and then stopping it, Gus." Poppy said, and the song in her voice had finished. Her words were ice.

"I never said I'd be drinking, woman." Gus said.

"Gus." Tom warned.

"Sorry bud, I just meant I'd come in and see you. Check

on ya. I have to walk past to get home pretty much. Just a bit of family concern."

"You'd have no family concern if he didn't live in a pub." Poppy said. Her eyes filled with tears and she stood up and began to clear the table, stacking plate on top of plate. Gus had a slice of pizza in his hand. She ripped it out of his fingers and added it to the pile. "You promised me this time you'd do it for real."

"It's not that easy." Gus said quietly.

"Look, let's leave you to it, eh?" Tom said.

Poppy stomped through to the kitchen and Sandy followed.

"I'm so sorry." Sandy said. "Shall I help you wash up?"

"No, no, it's fine, don't worry." Poppy said through her tears. "Just for once, I thought it'd be nice to try and be normal. Have people over. Relax and chat. I know it's my own fault. Every time he tells me he's going to stop, I believe him."

"He probably means it when he says it." Sandy said. "It can't be easy, giving it up."

"I know." Poppy said. "I do know that. That's why I'm so bloody patient. But I want my life back. I'm sick of living like this."

Sandy gave Poppy's arm a squeeze. "Why don't you go and have a hot bath and an early night? Everything seems worse at night. You'll be okay tomorrow."

"Yeah, I guess." Poppy said.

"You ladies okay?" Tom asked as he appeared in the kitchen doorway. "I told Gus to go for a walk and clear his head."

Poppy groaned. "Three guesses where he'll end up."

"Well, if he does that's his choice. It gets him out of your hair for a while, though."

She nodded. "I'm going to listen to your lovely lady's wise words and jump in the bath for a bit."

"Sounds good." Tom said. He pulled Poppy in for a hug. "Look, I know we don't talk every day or anything, but you're my sister and I love you. I'm always here for you, okay?"

"Me too." Sandy said.

Poppy pulled away from Tom's strong chest and smiled at them both. "Thank you. He just has these demons he needs to work through himself."

12

*V*ictor Dent's farmhouse was inaccessible thanks to the rain that had poured endlessly overnight. The field had transformed into a miserable bog and while Sandy's old Land Rover could get her as close as she wanted it to over the sodden terrain, she refused to tackle the rest of the way on foot, and reversed off the land before he saw her. Hopefully.

She dropped her speed and took the village bends slower than normal, splashing through huge puddles and flashing her lights frantically at an oncoming lorry with no headlights on. The shire horses stood, heads down, long manes matted with rain and mud, as she passed their field. On dry days, she often carried a spare carrot or two in the boot of her car and would park up, hop out and spend a pleasant few minutes stroking the animals before gifting them a carrot each.

No such luck today, horses, she thought, and was then overcome with so much guilt she was tempted to retrace the journey and stop after all.

The deafening noise of the rain battering down on the

car roof stopped her, and she continued her drive back in to the village. When she arrived at Books and Bakes, she would ring Victor and apologise for not turning up. She had no news, anyway. No developments. She felt dreadfully aware that she was becoming another person who had tried, and failed, to help him.

The car in front of her braked and she performed an emergency stop, her car swerving slightly. She managed to maintain control, though, and brought the car to a stop a few feet behind the Mini Cooper.

Between the bend in the road, the car ahead, and the heavy rain, she couldn't see what the hold up was. She drummed her fingers on the steering wheel until she noticed people moving around in the road ahead. With a groan, she pulled the hood of her yellow Mac over her head and pushed the car door open.

"Is everything okay?" She shouted ahead to make her voice heard over the rain.

A young woman stood, hands on hips, grey t-shirt soaked to her skin, looking ahead down the road. Sandy reached her and followed her gaze.

There was a man in the middle of the road, in the red football shirt and shorts he'd been wearing the night before.

"Oh, Jesus." Sandy said.

"I've called the police." The woman said, noticing Sandy.

"The police? I don't think that's necessary." Sandy scolded.

"Well, I didn't know what else to do. He can't stay out here." The woman said. She must have only just been old enough to drive.

Sandy sighed and ran past the woman and towards the man, who had tired himself out and sat on the dry stone wall muttering to himself.

"Gus?" She said.

He looked up at her, and she knew instantly that he was sober.

"You'll catch your death out here, come on. Let's get you into the car." Sandy said, pleased that her car was years' old and no longer precious to her to the extent that she begrudged the seats getting wet. Gus rose to his feet and she led him back up the hill towards her Land Rover.

"What are you doing?" The woman called.

"Getting him dry." Sandy said. She opened the passenger seat and Gus climbed in, then she returned to the young woman. "Do you want to take my details for when the police come?"

The woman blinked at her. "I need to get to work, I can't stay here..."

"Well, that's up to you, but he's soaked. He needs to go home and get dry and warm. He hasn't done anything wrong, he's free to leave."

"I just knew he needed help." The woman said, peering behind Sandy to the car. She dropped her voice. "Are you sure it's safe to take him in your car?"

"He's my brother-in-law." Sandy said. It was the first time she'd thought of him in such a way, and it made her stomach flip. Things with Tom must be serious if she was adopting his troubled relatives as her own.

"Oh, well, that's okay then. Well I'll wait for a few minutes for the police." The woman said. She pulled out her phone from her shorts pocket and took a photo of Sandy's name and number, held up on her own phone. "I hope he's okay."

"He's fine." Sandy said with a tight smile. Luckily, the woman was clearly from out of town, so there would be no gossip following on from the incident. But what on Earth had Gus been thinking?

She trudged back to her car and drove into the village, through the hammering rain, waiting for Gus to break the silence. He stared out of the window instead, his view nothing more than sheets of rain hitting the window with force.

"What's going on, Gus?" She asked finally as they entered Waterfell Tweed. Her village was ahead, on the left. She wished she'd stayed in bed for a lie in.

"I didn't know where to go." He said, and Sandy heard a desperation in his voice.

"You could have -"

"I can't go home. Not any more." Gus said.

"I don't think Poppy's kicked you out, Gus." Sandy said. Maybe Tom was more firm with him than he'd admitted, but Sandy couldn't imagine that he'd told Gus not to return.

"No, she hasn't." He said.

"Well? I'm sorry, I've not stuck my nose into your business before, but I need to know you're okay."

He sighed and his shoulders dropped. All of the tension seemed to disappear from his body. "I'm leaving her, alright? I can't keep doing this to her."

A chill ran through Sandy. "What do you mean? You can't leave Poppy. She's stood right by you all these years."

"Exactly. She'll be better off without me."

Sandy pulled to the side of the road and stopped the car. She glared at Gus. "Don't be silly. She loves you and she wants to help you. She'll be worried sick that you've been gone."

"That's the thing, she won't. I stay out so often she hardly notices."

"Trust me. She might not talk to you about it, but she worries."

"This'll stop her worrying, then." Gus said. There was no fight in his voice, Sandy realised. He had, quite simply given up. "I'll tell her, don't worry. I'm not gonna just disappear."

"Please think about it." Sandy urged as she moved the car back into the line of traffic. As much as she'd like to hold Gus hostage until he reconsidered, he desperately needed to get home and dry.

**

Sandy lost herself in the new book stock after dropping Gus at home.

The shop was empty, as was the cafe downstairs. Nobody was venturing out of their home unless they had to. Even Dorie was absent.

She turned the radio on and busied herself, checking the condition of each book and then scanning it into the cataloging software, before adding it to a pile on the other side of the computer. When the pile began to wobble dangerously, she got up and put each book in its new home.

The shop had become so popular that sourcing new second-hand stock was an ongoing job. Her weeks usually involved at least one trip to a private house clearance or an auction, or even a viewing at other bookshops that were going out of business.

Her favourite were the house clearances, where books that had often been forgotten about for decades were finally given a chance to find a new owner who would treasure them. Some of the clearances offered nothing of interest or value, but some of them revealed real gems; rare and antiquated books, signed first editions, even a few original manuscripts with an editor's suggestions marked up in long-faded red ink.

"Sandy?" A voice called as she slotted a book on demonology into the occult section.

"Victor?" She replied, recognising the old man's voice. She walked to the end of the aisle and saw him, stood by the till, a book in his hand. "Sorry, I didn't hear anyone come in. I thought everyone'd be indoors today."

"I saw you come and go, thought I'd better check you're okay." He said. His concern was touching to her, and the rawness of it made him shift on his feet. How long since he'd had someone to worry about?

"Sorry about that." She said. "I was only popping by to see if you were alright, and the land was so bogged down. I didn't have my wellies."

"Ah." He said, the disappointment palpable. "I thought maybe there was news."

"No, not yet, I'm afraid." She said. She thought of him driving back to the farmhouse, back to the silence of an empty house. "Why don't you have a breakfast while you're here? I could do with a break myself."

He smiled at her and handed the book across to her. It was a book on travel. Sandy recognised it from the display she had created to greet people as soon as they reached the top of the stairs. "I'll just take this, then get out of your hair."

"Are you going away?"

He laughed. "I've never been away in my life. I know I can't just pop in here and take up your time, though."

"Oh, Victor, you don't have to buy a book just because you're here. Don't be silly." She said and added the book to the next pile of books to add to the aisles. "Come on, let's go and have something to eat."

He didn't argue and she lead him downstairs, surprised by how well he managed the staircase.

The cafe was still empty and she caught Coral swiping at her phone again. *No phones* was one of the few rules Sandy insisted on. It looked so unprofessional and unwelcoming when customers walked in, to see staff engrossed in their phones. Coral blushed and returned her phone under the counter.

"Coral, can we have two full Englishes and two mugs of tea, please?" Sandy ordered. Coral nodded, relieved. Tea, she could manage. Bernice would take care of the food.

"My Travis loved a full English." Victor said with a far-off smile. Sandy wondered what it must be like to live in a world where everyday life was a sharp reminder of loss.

"Would you tell me about him?" She asked.

He grinned. An actual grin. "Nobody wants me to, normally."

Sandy smiled but wasn't sure that was true. Victor had isolated himself so well from a village of people who she was sure would want to hear his memories, if only to get a break from Dorie's endless chatter.

"He was an angel." Victor said. "There's never been a more perfect child, a more wonderful son. He couldn't do a thing wrong."

Sandy smiled.

"Anything I asked him, he did it right away. No back chat like other kids gave. He was like a little version of me. I mean, we spent so much time together, while Val tried to get herself right. We'd get our boots on and go off over the fields. He loved that. Loved being outside he did. I said to him like, whatever you want to do it's alright. And I hoped he'd want the farm, you know, of course I did, but it was his choice. And he always said yeah, he wanted the farm. Maybe he'd do some travelling first, that's all he said. Bit of travelling, then settle down at the farm. He never even got to travel, though."

Sandy reached across the table and squeezed his hand as Bernice appeared with two huge plates of English breakfasts.

"Blimey." Victor said as he eyed up the food. "I've not eaten this well in years."

"I piled on an extra sausage when I heard it were you out here, pet." Bernice said as she flashed a wink in Victor's direction. He grinned, revealing a mouth of mainly missing teeth.

"This'll go down a treat." He said. The plate was a mountain of fried eggs, beans, mushrooms, tomatoes, black pudding, bacon and sausages. Bernice reappeared a moment later with a side plate piled high with golden brown toast smothered in butter.

"Enjoy." She called and returned to the kitchen.

"Well, Sandy, it's no surprise why you're doing so well with food this good."

"You're always welcome, you know." Sandy said. She would love to see Victor join in village life, but he seemed determined to remain alone in the farmhouse. This, sitting down with him for a meal, was progress.

"It's hard to come out and enjoy myself when there's no justice for Travis." Victor explained as he stabbed a whole sausage with his fork and took a bite. He groaned involuntarily as he chewed. "Good quality meat, this is. Don't see that much anymore."

"It's all from the butcher." Sandy explained. She could save money buying meat from the wholesaler, but she wouldn't be able to say that it was local, high-quality meat if she did that. And her customers came back time after time because of how good her food was. A reputation could be lost in an instant.

"You've got a canny business head on you."

"I don't know about that." Sandy admitted. "I've made my share of mistakes."

"Haven't we all, eh." Victor said, lost to his memories once again.

*S*he heard the footsteps before the rap at the door.

The rain had finally stopped, and even the constant Waterfell Tweed wind had died down, creating an eerie quiet as Sandy finished tidying the cafe ready for the next day.

She'd told Bernice and Coral to head off home after they'd shared the washing up. Derrick had a rare day off to take his mum to a medical appointment. Sandy hadn't wanted to pry but the boy, and his mum, had been on her mind all day. She hoped nothing was wrong.

She added sending him a text message to her mental to-do list, which felt endless. She had so many new books to catalogue and put out on the shelves in the bookshop, and Bernice was about to leave for a fortnight's holiday. She was off gallivanting on a cruise around the Mediterranean, and Sandy was doing her best not to be jealous and failing miserably. She could just do with a couple of weeks lying on a sun lounger watching the ocean pass by, moving only to change into her best clothes for a plush meal prepared by someone else. Oh yes. Maybe she should suggest it to Tom. Another item added to her mental to-do list.

The tables gleamed, freshly wiped and cleaned. Menus stood proud on each table, together with a small vase with a single pink rose in. She replaced the roses weekly, much to Bernice's disapproval. An unnecessary expense, Bernice said. But they created a lovely smell.

The little touches made a difference. Sandy truly believed that.

She hoped that if the day ever came when one of the giant chains of coffee shops opened a branch in Waterfell Tweed, her customers would remain loyal to her. And she believed their loyalty would be as much down to the little personal touches as anything else.

She returned the salt and pepper shakers to the correct tables, wondering as she always did how one table ended up with three pepper grinders and no salt, while another table had neither and at least one salt shaker ended up on the carpet. If she didn't know better, she'd wonder if the cafe had a ghost who amused themselves with moving the objects around each day.

She looked up at the sound of the heels, and knew immediately that the woman was coming to see her. She felt her heart begin to race.

The rap on the door was short, determined, to the point.

The rap of a woman on a mission.

Sandy dropped the tea towel on the counter and unlocked the door.

"Valerie." She said. The woman wore a pale lilac blouse, trousers that appeared to be leather effect, and stiletto heels. It was as if every part of her was actively rebelling for the years she spent as a farmer's wife. "Come in... we're closed, but I'm guessing you're not here for food?"

"No, I'm not here for food." Valerie said. Her mouth was a stern, crimson line. She followed Sandy into the cafe, to the seating area, but remained standing.

"How can I help?"

"Word's reached me that you've been asking abut me. Me and my boy."

"I've been trying to work out what happened to him."

"What makes you think you're so special, then?" Valerie asked, eyes fierce. "The police try for 20 years and give up, but you think you can work it out? Are you some kind of genius?"

"Oh, no." Sandy said with a flustered laugh. "I'm definitely not a genius. I've solved a few murder cases, though."

"Really?" Valerie asked, a perfectly shaped eyebrow raised.

"Accidentally, at first. Someone was trying to frame me for a murder a while ago, I didn't have a choice really. I had to solve it. And since then, well..."

"You attract murders then, do you?"

"Sadly, it seems that way."

"And you really think you can work out what happened to Travis?" Valerie asked. She lowered herself into a seat and sat, ruler straight, as her defences began to collapse.

"Well." Sandy began. She had begun to doubt her ability to solve such an old case. A case so old, so cold, that even the police had given up on it. The last thing she wanted to do was give false hope to a woman who seemed to have found peace with the case remaining unsolved. "I don't know, if I'm honest."

"Victor thinks you can do it." Valerie said.

"I think he hopes I can." Sandy said. "I haven't promised him anything, you know. I said I'd try, and I have."

"Oh I know that. Well, I'm surprised you've not tried to speak to me before now."

"I didn't know if you'd want to speak to me." Sandy said.

"Oh, get. You've heard the rumours and thought I was too crazy to talk to." Valerie said.

Sandy froze, unsure how to react.

"I was crazy, it's okay. Enough people say it behind my back." Valerie said. "They don't call it that now, of course. So, come on, you're trying to get information. Ask me."

"Ask you?"

Valerie glared at her. "You ask me whatever you might damn well need to ask me if it helps find out what happened to my boy."

Sandy gulped. "Okay. Well, all we know at the moment is that it was a drowning. Even that's not 100%. The police were never able to say whether he died in the water, or was dead when he hit the water."

Valerie nodded, apparently emotionless.

"Ask me." She whispered.

Sandy sighed. "Victor said you were out in the caravan the night it happened. Did you hear anything unusual? See anyone coming or going?"

"Nobody came or went, ever. Travis didn't have friends over. He was embarrassed."

"About what?"

"About me, I should think." Valerie said with a grimace. "You'd call it postnatal depression now I reckon, but I don't know if that can last as long as this did. Maybe it can if it don't get helped. I couldn't be around him much. I'd sit with him for a bit, you know, watch tele maybe. It did get easier when he got older, stopped needing me so much. But still, he was a grown man and I was a mess."

"He was close to Victor?"

"As a lad." Valerie said with a quick nod. "He got more distant when he grew up."

"That's not what Victor remembers." Sandy said, as tactfully as she could.

"What does he remember?" Valerie asked. "I might have been unwell but my memory worked fine."

"He says that the two of them were still very close, that Travis never did anything wrong."

Valerie stifled a small grunt. "Well, is that so?"

"You don't agree?"

"I've still got his school reports, you know. They posted them out to me cos I never went to a parents' evening. Something happens to him, when he turns fourteen. You can see it, if you read them. And I do, I do read them. He's a quiet lad, but a good boy. And then he's fourteen and it all changes. Detentions, back chat, then it gets worse."

Sandy walked over to the counter and boiled the kettle, made two strong coffees and placed one in front of Valerie.

"He started wagging school, that's when the letters came out. The council got involved at one stage, said it was my job to make sure he was attending regularly. I couldn't even brush my teeth some days then, I don't know what they wanted me to do to a teenage boy taller than me."

"What happened?"

"Well, they came out and talked to us. Said he'd got in with a rum crowd. It were news to us cos he never had friends over. We thought he didn't have any. I'd always been a bit of a loner myself. I was too pretty, women didn't like me. So I thought he were just a loner like me."

Sandy took a sip of coffee, scalded her tongue, tried to hide the wince.

"Victor sat him down then, suggested he leave school and work on the farm."

"Leave school early?"

Valerie shrugged. "It made sense. He were inheriting a farm, he didn't need to do the tests like the other kids. He weren't interested though. Quite lazy by that point, he were. He saw the hours Victor worked and he didn't fancy that, so he buckled down. Scraped through some tests, did alright really, and then he went off to work in a factory."

"He didn't join the farm?"

"Nah, he listened to me for once about that. I told him to get out and see the world a bit, try other things. Farm life ain't easy. I wanted him to try other things first."

"So he'd had his spell of trouble and things settled down?"

"For a good while, yeah. Then he started stopping out. We thought he'd got a girl at first. He'd started knocking about with the rum 'uns from school again. A few of them, believe it or not, had been off to Uni. Then they came back and started knocking around again."

"Did he get in any trouble?"

"Oh no, he were a good lad. He'd been silly as a kid but he'd grown up, they all had. I think they played pool around someone's house, someone had a garage with a pool table, darts board. Nice place for a group of lads, it sounded."

Sandy sat quietly as Valerie took a sip of her coffee.

"I look back and I wish I'd done more, ya know. I wish I'd reached him. I mean, we had the space. We could have had a pool table in a barn, created a proper place for him and his mates. I do have a lot of regrets Sandy, I won't lie about that."

"You seem to be doing well now?"

"I found God." Valerie said. She instinctively reached for the gold cross around her neck. "He rescued me, and then I found the courage to see my doctor. I've not been a day off the tablets since, and they make the fog go away. I can see the world clear now. So, yeah, I'm doing good. Better than I deserve."

"What do you think happened to him?"

Valerie shrugged. "I've tried not to guess. I don't see what difference it'll make now, really. Won't change what happened."

"You know some people thought you'd done it." Sandy said. She watched the other woman's reaction carefully.

"Oh yeah." Valerie said with a wistful smile. "I'd probably have thought the same. Am I a suspect?"

"No, you're not." Sandy said. "I don't really have any suspects, to be honest."

"Well, you've gotta talk to the people who knew him. Don't talk to Victor, he only saw what he wanted to. And I guess I did the same. His friends, they're the people to talk to."

"I don't know where to start."

Valerie held her gaze for a moment. "I can help ya with that."

"You can?"

Valerie smiled. "I didn't sleep well back then. Seemed to spend all day and night like a zombie, never really asleep and never really awake. Heard a lot of things when people thought nobody was awake. There's a couple of names - Fuzzy and Bomber."

"Bomber?"

"Fuzzy and Bomber, they're the two I remember. Never saw either of them, but heard their names."

"That's a big help." Sandy said, even as her insides churned.

"Well, maybe I'm not totally useless." Valerie said. She took another sip of her coffee and stood up, using the table to push herself up to standing. "I'll let you get on. And Sandy?"

"Yes?"

"You'll tell me, won't you, if you find anything out?"

"Of course." Sandy promised. She held the door open and remained in the doorway long after Valerie had left.

She knew what she had to do next.

14

*T*he sweat poured down her forehead profusely.

A drop splashed into her eye, causing her to drop out of the pose and squeeze her eye shut. She clamped her hand over the eye and rubbed, which only spread the sweat into any corners of her eye that it hadn't already got into.

The stinging was intense and she bit her lip, then struggled to her feet and crept out of the pod as quietly as she could.

In the bathroom she splashed cold water into her eyes and pressed a paper towel against them.

By the time she left the toilet, the class had finished and only Cass remained, her skin dry and make-up intact.

"How do you do it?" Sandy asked, the affected eye still too painful to open. "How can you not sweat? It's unnatural."

Cass shrugged. "What can I say? God loves me."

"You shouldn't joke about the big fella while we're in his house." Sandy said, looking up at the roof ceiling.

"Oh yeah. Shoot." Cass said with a nervous laugh.

"Come on, let's get out of here. What happened to you anyway? And what's with the eye? Are you being a pirate?"

"You're hilarious." Sandy said as they walked out together into the frigid night air. "I managed to sweat so much it got in my eye. I've probably got your sweat glands as well as my own, knowing my luck."

Cass rolled her eyes. "Everyone's a hater when you have a beauty like mine."

"I've always liked your modesty."

"I've always liked your peg leg."

Sandy began to laugh and found that she couldn't stop. She would have to speak to Cass' boyfriend soon and accuse him of being involved in a murder, and yet she couldn't stop laughing. The more she tried, the more hysterical Cass' joke became, until Sandy bent doubled over and felt an ache shoot down her side.

"Ooh, I've got stitch!" Sandy squealed in between giggles, and Cass began to laugh too.

Five minutes later, when Olivia locked up the church, the two of them were hanging on to the church gate laughing hysterically.

"What on earth's got into you two?" Olivia asked, the most mature one present and not even old enough to order a pint.

Neither could answer her, and she shook her head and walked past them. "I'm going to Derrick's tonight, don't wait up."

Cass stopped laughing immediately. "Nice try lady, you know the curfew."

Olivia rolled her eyes but nodded. She was a good kid.

"Oh, I needed that laugh." Sandy said as she regained composure.

"You definitely did." Cass said. "You need to relax more, Sand."

"Easier said than done." Sandy said. "I've got so much to do, it's endless."

"No it isn't." Cass said with a shrug. "It's only as endless as you let it be. You're the boss, remember. You make the decisions."

"Yeah, I guess." Sandy said. She felt the distance between the two of them, the things she couldn't say. The suspicion she couldn't raise.

"Why don't you come to the salon, I'll do you a quick massage?" Cass asked, and as tempting as the offer was, all Sandy could feel was the sweat still sticking to her.

"I couldn't inflict this sweat on your massage beds." Sandy said with a smile.

"Ew, you dirty bint, I meant after a shower!" Cass exclaimed, and Sandy began to laugh again.

"Do you know what, I think I'll take you up on that. Give me half an hour?"

**

Cass had the hands of a magician.

She managed to find all of the tension in Sandy's body which apparently wasn't hard as there was so much of it. Starting in a ball at the base of her spine, the knots were throughout her back and across to her shoulders. Cass worked each one out in turn while classical music played out in the background.

"Now just close your eyes and relax." Cass said as she applied more oil to her hands. "That's an order."

Sandy didn't argue.

She closed her eyes and resisted the urge to make small talk, to check how Cass was doing, or to feel guilty for all of the productive things she could have been doing with the time instead.

She lay back and allowed her mind to drift.

She was close to the truth, she could sense it.

The facts were there, the pieces were just beyond her vision, calling out to her. She could almost sense Travis himself, reaching out to her, waiting for her to catch up. Waiting for her to put it all together.

15

---

*I*t was almost a week since the police had closed the case, and Sandy woke from a deep sleep with a nervous energy coursing through her veins.

The Cat sat on the windowsill, looking outside. She pulled herself up out of bed and followed his gaze.

Jim stood on his drive, a backpack in his hand. The car boot was already full. Elaine stood close to him, arms folded.

"No, Jim, just let me have some time." Sandy heard Elaine's words come through the open window.

"Oh, no." Sandy murmured. She ducked back down into bed, not wanting to spy on them.

"Elaine, please. Let me explain. Just give me a few more days?"

"I can't, Jim. I've been patient enough. Come back in a couple of days." Elaine said. Sandy heard the car door open, then close, and then the engine roar into life.

When she glanced out of the window again, a few moments later, the car had gone and Elaine remained outside, looking lost.

"I'd better go and check on her." Sandy told The Cat, who looked unmoved by their neighbours' plight. She pulled on jeans and a baggy t-shirt and took the stairs two at a time, hair and teeth unbrushed.

"Elaine?" She called out from the front door. "I'm just boiling the kettle if you want a drink."

Elaine turned to her and shook her head. "I just need some time."

"Everything will work itself out."

"I know." Elaine said. "I just can't have him under my roof acting so strange."

"Well, the offer's there if you want it. I've took the day off work so I'll be home all day."

"Kind of you Sandy, but I'll be alright once I get this sorted."

She nodded and closed the door.

She'd sent Bernice a message the night before, after her massage, advising that she'd be taking the day off. Completely off. As in, she planned to leave her phone in a drawer somewhere and do nothing but relax. It was her last chance before Bernice's cruise.

There was just one thing she needed to do first.

She picked up her phone and dialled the number, listened to the rings until it went to a voicemail that hadn't been personalised.

"It's me. I need to talk to you, about Travis Dent. I'll be at home all day. Come and see me today." She said in her most stern voice, hoping the nerves she felt weren't audible in the message.

And then, she went into the kitchen and made herself a creamy mug of mocha. She took it into the living room and sat in the chair nearest the window, and focused on the silence.

She didn't even feel like reading.

It felt as if she was in quiet contemplation, almost religious in its intensity. She was preparing, she knew. Preparing for a final showdown.

Preparing for answers she didn't think she'd like.

Waterfell Tweed was going to be changed forever, she could sense it.

And then her doorbell rang.

**

He shifted his weight from one foot to the other, one foot to the other, until she stood aside and let him in.

"I know what this is about." He said as he paced down the hallway into her kitchen. The kitchen was tiny, but it never looked smaller than it did then, as he stood there, larger than life, energy erupting from his every pore.

"Come and talk in here." She said, gesturing to the living room, but he stood his ground in the kitchen.

"I know what you think I did, but you've gotta trust me, I didn't hurt him." He said, and he sounded so sincere. She so wanted to believe him.

"But you knew him?"

"Course I did." He said. "Everyone knew him."

"Do you know what happened to him?"

"He drowned." Bomber said with a shrug. "That was the word on the street."

"There's more to it, you know that." Sandy said.

Bomber paced back towards her, then turned on his heel and paced back to the kitchen. "I dunno. Nobody knows what happened. It was tragic, I know that."

"Tell me what you know."

Bomber buried his head in his hands. "God, I've tried to move past all that. We was in the same circle for a bit. He was older than me, man. I was a kid. Thought it'd be cool to hang around with that lot."

"Did you know him?"

"Nah. Like I say, I was a kid. Tryin'a be a tough guy."

"Was it a bad crowd?"

"Yeah, yeah it was." Bomber said. "I dunno if you'll remember it, there were a lot of burglaries happening around then. It were this gang doing 'em. I didn't do anything, just tagged along for a bit."

"Travis' mum said she'd heard your name."

"Yeah, she would have." Bomber said with a sigh. "They pulled this prank on me. The idiots. Set me up good they did, this was before Cass. They told me they'd found me a girl, said she wanted to meet me... for a date, like. I turn up at the place and she never shows, but those morons are all there in the bushes killing themselves. She didn't even exist. It were pathetic. These were grown men, you know? Getting off on teasing a kid like that. I didn't have anything to do with them after that. That's why my name woulda come up."

Sandy nodded. She could imagine girl-mad Bomber standing out in the park for a mysterious girl to arrive. And she could imagine his fury when it turned out to be a prank.

"Did Travis have anything to do with that?"

Bomber shrugged. "How would I know? I didn't stick around to ask who had the great idea. I doubt it though, he wasn't involved much. He was on the side, like. He turned up sometimes for smokes, when his own money were low. But he had a job, most of 'em didn't, so he weren't involved in much."

"Was he involved in the burglaries?"

"Nah, I don't reckon so." Bomber said. "Look, Sand, I know I've made my mistakes, but I'd never hurt anyone. And the police know all about this. They spoke to me about the 999 call and I told 'em everything."

"What 999 call?"

"Someone reported it, when he fell in the river."

"I didn't know that." Sandy said. "They found out who made that call?"

"I couldn't tell ya. It all went quiet. Word was that Simmons had shut it down, ya know, brushed it under the carpet."

"Why would he do that?" Sandy asked, her stomach churning. She was so close.

"Well, to protect his nephew, like."

"Let me guess. Is his nephew Fuzzy?"

Bomber's face blanched, but he nodded.

16

He was exactly where Bomber had told her he would be.

The riverbank was empty apart from him, camped out on a folding chair, a two-man tent erected behind him. A cool box stood open by his side, with nothing inside.

He hardly responded when he saw her. A slight tilt of his head to acknowledge her, nothing more.

"I've only got one chair." He called out to her.

She had knee boots on and she was glad for them as she made her way through the long grass.

"Fuzzy?" She said and the man gave a nod.

"I wondered how long it'd be." He said.

"You could have ran away further." She said with a light smile.

"I'm not running." He said. "It's important that people know that. I do have some sense of right and wrong, you know."

"Of course you do." She said. Bizarrely, she didn't doubt that. "Do you want to tell me what happened?"

"It was stupid." He said. "I was trying to act tough. You

know, when your family's full of police, you grow up being good and doing the right thing. I guess I wanted to be the bad guy. The bad guys seemed to get the girls."

He coughed and then fell silent, lost with his thoughts.

"I never did a thing wrong, just hung around with a few big talkers. They reckoned they were doing all these burglaries. I never believed it. Then one of 'em came back and told us about this job he were planning. An armed robbery. That's when I knew they were all full of crap."

He spoke slowly, reliving it. "They came looking for me the next day, the lads did. They'd done it. It was all over the news. Armed robbery at a corner shop."

"I think I remember that." Sandy said. A flash of an Asian woman talking to journalists about the terror she'd felt appeared in Sandy's mind.

"They showed me the money. Offered me some. I was lucky to get a fiver a month at home, what was I meant to say? They gave me fifty quid and I thought I was a big man, then. The next night they were talking about training me up, saying I were a hard man, and I lapped it up. I've never been a hard man in my life, always been a bit soft, I'd have listened to them talk about me like that all day long. Never had any intentions of doing anything."

He sighed and his voice became less steady.

"That's how they got me. The group, it were like one or two nutters, and the rest were just bored lads like me looking for summit to do. It weren't a bad crowd. I played along, said yeah I'd do the next one. There were no chance it'd ever happen. Then Travis, he got the spooks. They were planning the next one, but they'd picked out this place, said it were full of money. I never realised till later, it were his farm. The Dent farm."

"Oh God." Sandy said, picturing Travis, caught between two worlds.

"He stormed off and said he were ringing the police, and that's what did it. That's what cost him his life. The stupid moron. All he had to do were walk off quiet and then ring 'em. But no, he had to say that's what he were planning."

"And then what happened?" Sandy coaxed.

"They told me, it were my time to step up. Said he needed taking out and I had to do it."

"Taking out?"

"Killing." The man said, and he closed his eyes. "They said he needed killing. To shut him up, like. It was a test. They knew I had police in the family, that's why they called me Fuzzy, so they were checking if I were really on the level."

"Wow." Sandy said.

"I caught up with him, told him the others were morons, talked him into having a drink with me. I didn't know what to do, Sandy. I was just a kid. We went up to the bridge, took some vodka. I'd never really drank before, that's how green I was. We just sat there drinking. He were a nice lad, ya know. I'd never really spoke to him before. He told me about the farm, said his mum were a bit crazy. I told him they'd sent me to kill him and he laughed. Everything were funny at that point, we'd had so much to drink. He knew I weren't gonna hurt him. I said he'd make my life a lot easier if he'd just jump. So he did."

"He jumped?"

"I never laid a finger on him." The man said. "He was too drunk to understand. He just saw it as a dare, I reckon, I said jump and he did. Even when he stood up, I didn't realise. I didn't think he'd do it. He went with such a splash. It were pitch black, and I'm no swimmer. I ran, found the nearest phone box and..."

"You rang 999?"

He nodded. "I ran home after that. That was my mistake. I should have stayed. I should have stuck around. I just told them I'd been by the river and heard a splash, sounded big enough to be a person."

"I don't know what to say." Sandy said. "How have you lived with this for so long, Gus?"

The butcher looked at her, and his face was the answer. His ruddy complexion, his puffy eyes, the near-constant slurring of his words. She remembered Poppy's words. He has his demons.

"I got him drunk that night, and I ain't never stopped drinking since." He said.

"Nobody knows?"

He shook his head. "I hid for weeks after. The other lads, they thought I was the real deal after that. I didn't want any part of it. I've never told anyone."

"Your uncle, he doesn't know?"

Gus leaned his head back, stretched the muscles in his neck. "I reckon he might have had a feeling, but we've never talked about it. I know I need to be punished, Sandy. I'm ready."

"This is why you've left Poppy."

He nodded. "She don't deserve this. I've already put her through too much."

"I'll have to call the police, you know."

"I'm ready."

17

*S*andy was surprised to rediscover how much she enjoyed running the cafe in Bernice's absence. She'd given her strict instructions to switch off from work and enjoy the break, and take lots of photographs. Bernice had assured her that she'd manage to do that, and Sandy had slipped into long working days, opening up the cafe in the morning, working front of house all day long, and then devoting her evenings to cataloguing the book stock.

Tom had surprised her a few evenings by turning up and ordering her to put him to work, which was frankly a situation she could get used to. His strong arms made quick work of putting all of the books out in the right places, leaving her to check the condition of the books and upload them to the stock tracker.

The system told her that she had 4,800 books in stock, a number that blew her mind. She thought back to the shop's humble beginnings in her mind, when she had scoured charity shops and auctions for cheap books and stored them in her cottage before renting a storage unit. Her dream had well and truly come true, and she had amazing people around her, supporting her at every turn.

"Penny for them?" Tom asked as he returned to the till.

"I was wondering if I could buy you a drink." Sandy said with a smile.

"Are you asking me on a date, Sandy Shaw?"

"I think I might just be, Tom Nelson."

He looked at his watch and the darkening sky outside. "Well, I think it's the best offer I'll get today."

She punched his arm playfully. "Cheeky toad. You can buy me a drink instead, for your cheek."

"Come on then." He said.

They left the few remaining books and turned out the lights, locked up, and headed the few doors down the road to The Tweed.

Sandy had forgot that the football was on, again.

"Is this tournament over soon?" Sandy asked.

"It's the semi-final." Tom said, which didn't give the full answer he thought it did. "England in a semi-final, I never thought I'd see the day."

"You're not as young as you like to pretend, Tom."

"No, I'm serious. This has never happened in my life-time." He said.

"Oh." Sandy said, realising why the match was such a big deal. "This must be amazing for business."

"It certainly is." Tom said with a grin. He lead her into a booth table. "What shall I get us to drink?"

"I'll have a white wine." Sandy said. She surveyed the pub, which was full of familiar faces.

"I'd really rather just stay at home." Elaine's familiar voice came from behind Sandy. Sandy peered over to see Elaine and Dorie sitting in the next booth along. "Oh, hello Sandy."

"Evening, ladies." Sandy said.

"Tell her, Sandy, she can't sit at home moping. She needs to get out." Dorie said. She was dressed to the nines, in a long velvet dress that showed a little more cleavage than Sandy thought was strictly necessary, even if England were in the semi-final.

"I just fancied a night at home." Elaine said. stirring the straw in her orange juice.

"Well, you'll be glad you came out. It's a momentous night."

"It's coming home!" A man roared as he burst in with a group of friends, all kitted out in the England football kit.

"Ugh, it's so noisy." Elaine moaned. She looked thoroughly miserable.

"Here you go." Tom said as he returned to their table with a white wine and a pint of dark ale. "Cheers!"

"What are we celebrating?" Sandy asked. She hadn't felt like celebrating since she'd watched the police cart Gus Sanders away following their riverbank discussion. "England haven't won yet."

"They're not taking any action against Gus." Tom said with a grin.

"What? Are you kidding?" Sandy asked, mimicking his smile.

"They've listened to everything that happened and they're satisfied it was an accident. Just a really tragic accident."

"Wow." Sandy said. "I didn't think it could be murder. It was an accident, you're right. Have you seen Gus?"

"He's having a quiet night in with Poppy."

"Ah, good. How's she doing?"

"I don't know if they'll make it." Tom said with a shrug.

"She's gonna need some time to get her head around what he was hiding from her."

"It's such a sad case. I can't help thinking his uncle would have been better to do things properly and tell Gus all those years ago that he wasn't responsible."

Tom shrugged. "We can't change what happened."

"But look at the heartache it's cost everyone - Victor and Valerie, Gus..."

"How did Victor and Valerie take the news?"

"It's the best news I could hope for." Victor's rumble of a voice came from beside them. He had put on his best jumper, free from holes, and a flat cap that looked relatively clean. He cupped a pint of Guinness in his hands.

"Victor!" Sandy exclaimed. "Come and take a seat."

"You'll be seeing a bit more of me, I reckon." He said as he sat across from them. "I never wanted to hide away, but I didn't know who to trust. I couldn't risk coming down here and being friendly to the person who hurt my boy."

"Does it feel better now, knowing that nobody hurt him?"

"I had visions of him being pushed. Or being hurt already before he even got in the water. I couldn't stand the thought of him being hurt. This is... it's... it's not okay. It'll never be okay. But I can get my head around it."

"That's a good start." Tom said. He reached across and patted Victor's arm. The old man smiled across at him.

"Not sure I can afford these prices, though. Extortionate. Who's the landlord?"

Tom began to laugh, realised that Victor wasn't joking, and laughed harder.

"Can I have your attention?" A voice came then from the bar. Bomber. Sandy looked at Tom, who shrugged. "We've got a few minutes before the big kick off, and someone's asked to have everyone's attention. Have we got Elaine Peters in here? Elaine, can you come forward?"

Sandy spun around in her seat in time to see Elaine's cheeks flush scarlet. She stood up, encouraged by Dorie who practically pushed her out of her chair.

"Here she is, round of applause for Elaine, who is of course the patron saint of Waterfell Tweed and lets Dorie Slaughter live with her!"

"Enough of your cheek, young man." Dorie called across to Bomber.

The door to the living quarters opened and in walked Jim, dressed in a pale grey suit. He held a microphone and walked across the room to Elaine, who stared at him in disbelief.

"I need to say sorry to you, that's the first thing. I know I've been acting strange. And I have been hiding something."

Elaine glanced behind her, away from Jim.

"I've been secretive, I've been different. And it's because I've been nervous. I didn't know how to do... this." Jim said, and he dropped to one knee. He pulled a small jewellery box from his trouser pocket, opened it to reveal a gold ring, and gazed up at Elaine, who had begun to sob.

"Elaine Peters, you're the most wonderful woman I've ever met, right up there on the same level as my mum. I want to spend the rest of my life with you, and I promise I'll never act strange again like I have been recently. So, would you do me the honour of being my wife?"

Elaine's subtle mascara lay in trails down her cheeks, and as she sobbed, she nodded frantically. Jim staggered to his feet, time slowing for a moment as he appeared to lose balance and looked at risk of toppling over on to the beer-soaked floor. He pulled Elaine in for a hug and when they separated, the mascara was all over his pale shirt.

It was the most unglamorous, perfect proposal Sandy could imagine.

"Three cheers for my son!" Dorie called from her seat.

"And the bride-to-be, Dorie?"

"Well, I suppose." Dorie said, but she flashed a smile.

The pub erupted in the toast for the happy couple, and then everyone's attention turned to the television.

It was a life-changing night.

**

Tom walked Sandy home, a little unsteady on his feet. She draped her arm through his and enjoyed the feel of him so close to her, so unguarded and silly.

"You're happy." She murmured to him.

"How could I not be?" He asked. "Jim and Elaine are enough to warm the cockles of anyone's heart."

"How adorable was he?" Sandy said.

"Would you like me to do that for you?"

"In the whole pub? No thanks!" Sandy said.

"Not there necessarily. Just generally, we've not really talked about the future, have we... other than saying we want to have a future together."

"What more is there to talk about?" Sandy asked, trying to keep the tone light.

"Babies, weddings, more cats?"

"Now probably isn't the time for this talk." She said with a smile.

"I'm not drunk enough to say anything I don't mean,

Sand. I mean, we're not getting any younger…"

"Thanks."

"You know what I mean. We should be able to talk about this stuff."

"Okay, what do you want in the future?"

"I want it all." He said with a grin as his footing missed the pavement and he stumbled down into the road. Sandy managed to keep him upright.

"Head in the clouds, feet in the gutter." She joked.

"I've always wanted to get married." He said, undeterred. He was having this conversation whether Sandy liked it or not.

"I guess I have too." Sandy said. "But I'd accepted it wouldn't happen for me. I always wanted children too."

"It's not too late." Tom said.

"You want kids?"

"I think so." He said.

"I don't think it's the kind of thing you do on a think-so, Tom. They don't come with a refund option."

"Ha ha." Tom said. "Sandy, you are serious about this, aren't you?"

"Of course I am, why?"

"It just feels like you hold back sometimes."

"I think it's all so unexpected, that's all. I'd just accepted I was single and that's the way it was probably going to stay."

"Well, I'm asking you to think about these things, okay." He said, suddenly serious. "We don't have to talk about them now. But I want to talk about them soon."

"Okay." She agreed. "I can do that. In fact…"

She reached into her handbag and held her hand out to him. "Why don't we start with this?"

"What is it?" Tom asked, looking at the object dumbly.

"A spare key, to mine." Sandy said. "I've been meaning to

give it you for a while, but you got ill and I was distracted... so, sorry it's late."

"Ah... so you do think about these things after all?"

"Yes." She admitted. "And we'll talk about it all, soon. I promise."

"I could creep in your cottage at night and watch you sleep." Tom said with a grin.

"Erm... weirdo. I'll have my key back if you keep talking like that!" Sandy said. Tom pulled her to him suddenly and planted a kiss on her lips. He tasted of beer and sweat and something that Sandy couldn't name, something that was just... him. She closed her eyes and allowed him to hold her, forgetting how unsteady he was for a moment, until they both toppled over the dry stone wall behind them and into the field.

They laughed for what felt like hours, and despite every part of Sandy's nature telling her to stand up and walk home, the night was warm and the sky was clear, and she lay in the field with the man she loved, drifting between sleep and mutterings of love until the sun rose.

"Sandy Shaw, is that you?" A familiar voice called over the wall. Sandy peeled herself away from Tom, who she had curled up into to hug in her sleep, and saw Rob Fields looking over the wall at her. Trust her to get caught sleeping in a field by the vicar.

"Rob! Good morning!" She called, doing her best attempt to sound sensible. "Beautiful day."

"It certainly is." Rob said. He looked down at Tom, still asleep, chin moist where he had dribbled on himself. "Is he okay?"

"A little worse for wear probably but he's fine." Sandy said. She nudged Tom, but he made no response other than a loud snore.

"I'll help you move him." Rob said. "He shouldn't stay down there, he'll get cold. I'll have to be quick though, I've got a busy day."

"The church is buzzing with all of Olivia's grand plans, hey?" Sandy asked as the two of them pulled Tom to his feet.

"Well, yes, but that's not what I'm up to today. I've got an apparently urgent meeting with Dorie Slaughter... something about wedding planning?"

"Oh, gosh... she moves quick." Sandy said with a laugh.

"I didn't even know she was dating." Rob said, perplexed.

Sandy grinned. "I'll let her fill you in."

**

Sandy put Tom to bed and took a quick shower. She had a busy day ahead of her too.

A full day in the cafe. The last books to sort.

And a trip to the doctor.

She hadn't told Tom. Hadn't wanted him to feel guilty that she'd caught his sickness bug.

She'd told herself it would clear after a day or two, but it persisted.

Every morning began with a race to the bathroom to throw up.

Something was wrong, she knew.

Either that, or something was very, very right.

THE END

GET-IN-MY-BELLY WAFFLES

To make the perfect waffles, you'll need a waffle maker.

To begin, switch on the power of your waffle maker so the machine begins to warm up.

Also, prepare your toppings. Sandy recommends fresh strawberries (bonus points if they're hand-picked, you know what a food snob she is!) and honey, but you can also try these combinations:

- Blueberries and clotted cream
- Raspberries and maple syrup
- Sliced banana and chocolate sauce
- Chopped apple and cinnamon
- Yoghurt and chia seeds
- Ricotta, mascarpone and mixed berries (stir together 1/2 cup ricotta and 1/2 cup mascarpone with 1 tbsp caster sugar)
- Peanut butter, banana and bacon

- Spinach, egg and cheese
- Apple and pecan

Ingredients:

2 x eggs
    250g x plain flour
    415ml milk
    120ml vegetable oil
    1 tbsp sugar
    4 tsp baking powder
    1/4 tsp salt
    1/2 teaspoon vanilla extract*
    **

Method:

1 Preheat the waffle maker if you haven't already

2 Beat the eggs in a large bowl until fluffy, then beat in flour, milk, vegetable oil, sugar, baking powder, salt and vanilla extract

3 Scoop the mixture into the waffle iron until it covers all of the ridges on the bottom iron. Do not overfill - be prepared to clean up if you do! Close the waffle maker and cook for between 4-7 minutes. Sandy recommends 7 minutes, for perfectly browned get-in-my-belly waffles

* Be like Sandy's mum and buy good-quality vanilla extract.

** A fan of savoury waffles? Try adding chopped bacon and cheese to the batter mix for a tasty savoury waffle!

WANT MORE COZY CONTENT?

If you're a lover of cozy mysteries, join my VIP Reader List.

Every Thursday, I send out an eMail packed with updates on my writing progress and life, plus special cozy mystery offers, free gifts, exclusive content and more.

Sign up now:

http://monamarple.com/wt7/

ABOUT THE AUTHOR

Mona Marple is a mother, author and coffee enthusiast. She is creator of the Waterfell Tweed cozy mystery series and the Mystic Springs paranormal cozy mystery series.

You can see all of her books at author.to/MonaMarple

When she isn't busy writing a cozy mystery, she's probably curled up somewhere warm reading one.

She lives in England with her husband and daughter.

Connect with Mona:
www.MonaMarple.com
mona@monamarple.com

facebook.com/MonaMarpleAuthor

twitter.com/MonaMarple

instagram.com/MonaMarple

Made in the USA
Las Vegas, NV
04 July 2024

91875072R00080